THE FIELDS

by Sammi Leigh Melville

Table of Contents

1

The Fall

The day would officially begin with the unearthing of an elbow, an ear, a foot; a group of children would stumble across one of these prized possessions and begin to dig, peeling the mud away in hopes that the elbow would become an arm, the ear a head, the foot a leg. With increased effort, the body parts would lead to a body. This dazed being, usually a child, would be coaxed out of the mud by its proud saviors, who would giggle and whisper to each other in glee; the newcomer would then be escorted to the bathhouse by an adult.

It was always the little ones who were first to run onto the field, feet struggling against the mud's sucking pull, eyes searching for the rare individuals who already protruded from the ground. They loved the game of it, the fun of discovering new playmates in the mud. The adults had a different mindset as they methodically followed, one eye watching the children running out ahead of them and the other nervously scanning the sky for the winged specters. To them, digging the fields was an act of duty and necessity.

Just at the perimeter of the field, Marie Goodwin began her patrol. There was hardly ever anything that she needed to watch over — crime was low in a village where there wasn't much to steal, where everyone knew everyone and would not consider hurting anyone unless it was a foreigner — but watch she did, day in and day out, her baton safely tucked into the folds of her cotton blue dress just in case. It was her duty as Sheriff.

And there was the business of watching the specters. Their lithe, ghostly bodies gave the semblance of a small human but had the wings of a bat, diaphanous but strong and powerful, with raking talons, and razor-sharp teeth jutting from their snarls. Gliding lazily over the field of mud, they glowed an ethereal blue even in the daylight. The beasts thought they owned the place — and perhaps they did, in a way. Several circled overhead right now, flexing their talons, a constant reminder that an attack could occur at any given moment against these innocent humans residing in the village.

But they remained in the sky, which was just where Marie would rather. And so she returned her gaze to the field, that lot of mud in which the Southern Village's diggers so avidly worked, spanning nearly a quarter of a mile. They scooped handful after handful of the thick, clumpy, slippery mess and tossed it into piles behind them, watching the mud sink back into the hole they had just created — but a little progress was still made. The diggers averaged about five rescues a month, though they saw plenty more under the mud than that... the field, however sacred the villagers considered it, acted like a petulant child: it was jealous of its captives, and liked to give the diggers glimpses of them, revealing a foot or a shoulder but, as soon as more help came, sucking it back down into its depths, teasing the diggers in an ever-so-coy (but ever-so-irritating) way. And so the whole village would rejoice when they finally managed to unearth a newcomer from its grasp.

Marie swallowed the sigh that inevitably came to her lips during her daily patrol. Truth be told, she couldn't stand the sight of the field; it sometimes struck her that this community of beautiful people wasted their days living in servitude to the needs of the field. Day after day they returned, breaking their backs and risking their lives to pry others from its grasp... they didn't have to, but Marie saw the guilty conscience of the collective people, saw

3

that they could not just sit back and let others lie unconscious underneath the mud, unable to open their eyes to the sunshine and stretch their legs on solid ground. No one with the same origins would wish that on anyone else... after all, what if the village had given up before they, themselves, were pulled from the mud? No, it was good that they fulfilled their duty; but still, Marie found herself secretly wishing the field wasn't there — that they could live in peace without knowledge of it. Or better yet, that it could be destroyed.

She gave a little shudder, amazed that the thought had even crossed her mind. Those thoughts were sacrilege. And besides, destruction was exactly what this village didn't need more of.

Marie caught a glimpse of Cecilia out on the field, gleefully helping the diggers, and a smile slowly edged its way back onto her face. Cecilia had been begging her to let her dig since she was four years old. "Mama, it's just mud! Mama, all the other kids got a chance. Mama, *I know how to dig.*" Of course, initially Marie had refused — there would be too many whispers from the villagers about a flesh-born child running loose on the field. There was only so much Marie could do to shield her daughters from the spite of the villagers — defying the very act of creation that the field itself performed and being born of another womb was a direct violation of the village's stasis, and was why some villagers even referred to these children as bastards — but she could at least curb the spark of controversy by not sending them onto holy ground. Even the field seemed to agree; it was too dangerous for flesh-borns to try their hand at digging, especially with the specters watching so closely. While everyone felt the inherent risk of falling back under the mud, it was rare for a flesh-born child to make it past three years old without being knocked under, no matter what pains the parents took to prevent it.

Marie shuddered at the memory of the last flesh-born child to fall, two years ago: a specter had swooped down out of the sky and snatched little Sandy from the safety of his own front yard, flown to the center of the field, and simply dropped him. The field had devoured him within seconds, though the diggers spent hours trying to get him back. The villagers had eventually made their peace with the incident — after all, though the child had not come from the field, he was finally able to connect with the village's collective Womb on some level — but the thought of it still made Marie instinctively want to scoop Cecilia up in her arms and hold her tight.

But Cecilia was a tough child. The first time, only just a month ago, she had snuck onto the field against her mother's wishes. And of course Marie found out, scrounging up enough of her silent fury — not only at Cecilia for disobeying her, but also at Mukisa, Cecilia's older sister by twelve years, who was supposed to have been watching her. But by the time she had run out to Cecilia's spot on the field to give her a talking to, Cecilia had pulled up a little girl. You had to give it to her... she seemed to have a natural knack for digging, regardless of the heightened bounty that the specters sought for her kind. It brought a swell of pride to Marie's chest — *her daughter, a digger*.

A good number of villagers had to admit that, the stigma of illegitimate birth aside, the Goodwin family had a knack for everything they put their minds to. Mukisa was the finest hunter the village had seen for years; and Cecilia clearly would be a fine digger when Marie ascertained that she should dig full time. The jobs they had so deftly picked up certainly held the skeptics at bay; their greatest defense from their neighbors' spite was to earn their respect. Marie's position perhaps helped heighten that respect to some extent: she had hesitantly taken her position as sheriff when the previous sheriff, Lucas Clarke, had passed on; now here she was, twenty years later, and she could barely have a conversation about taking another vote for the position without people getting upset. Marie smiled at the thought of what one of the elders, Mama Nina, had said just a few days ago: "Marie, you are a strong-hold, born to mother whatever lost soul came across your path. You didn't have kids, so you figured you'd mother an entire village.

And then Mukisa and Cecilia came along, and you just kept on doing a good job with the rest of us."

Out on the field, Cecilia hunched over a section of mud intently, her gaze fixed on something. With a muddied hand, she pushed the tight curls out of her face, uncompromising in her scrutiny of the ground before her. Marie shielded her eyes from the sun to get a better look as Cecilia's hand shot forward, reaching for something just under the surface of the mud; she looked up at the diggers around her, a smile spreading across her face. Shouting and motioning to those closest to her, she returned to her work with new vigor: she had excavated a hand.

The diggers around her smiled, nodding in approval at Cecilia, though they stuck to their own sections, hoping that they, too, could find a body part. Already Cecilia was showing up some of the most experienced diggers today… Marie could understand why they did not rush to her side to assist. Nobody wanted to be beaten by a seven-year-old, let alone a flesh-born seven-year-old. But Cecilia kept at it, and in a moment's time, Marie saw a head peeking out of the mud: a young boy's head, she could see. Now they would help her… getting the head to surface was half the battle, and the field would now be putting up a real fight.

But before Cecilia could even announce her victory, the head jerked back down into the mud. Cecilia stared in shock as the boy disappeared before her eyes, and plunged her hands into the mud around her, trying to find him.

Marie squinted, trying to make sense of the scene. Suddenly she saw a muddy hand shoot out of the space in front of Cecilia, and desperately grab hold of her arm — and then Cecilia lurched forward, screaming, yanked headfirst into the mud.

"Cecilia!" Marie bolted onto the field, making a beeline to the spot where her daughter had been. Other diggers who had seen the incident shouted and began reaching down, struggling to find her receding body in the mud. Marie shoved past them and reached her own arm down, into the slimy mess, into the heart of the field. Her fingers frantically clawed at the mud, grasping at nothing, over and over, and her heart began to climb into her throat.

After a while, Marie felt strong arms around her waist, pulling her away from the mud. It was possible that she kicked a man square in the jaw — she wasn't sure, but she didn't care — and the next thing she knew, she was on the edge of the field, seated on a tree stump and surrounded by people, a sea of comforting hands and a tangle of hushed words and everything was spinning and it was getting hot and the front of her dress was caked in mud and I'm sorry, Marie, but Cecilia is gone.

♦

Mukisa peeked through the the trees and smiled at the man before her, perched on a rock and minding his own business. Paul liked to have some time to himself, and she didn't usually like to disturb him… well, *sometimes* she liked to disturb him, but after her mother had lectured the two of them that their responsibilities should come before their personal lives, it was now more often than not that the disturbance was due to inevitability: she would be tracking a deer, or maybe a pheasant, and follow it right into his path, and suddenly she would see him there, off in his own little world. Not that he wasn't hunting — Mukisa knew that Paul was a great hunter — he just liked being alone sometimes.

Today must be one of those times. A particularly clever shaft of sunlight navigated past the shade of the oak trees and fell in Paul's general vicinity, allowing the man enough light with which to sharpen his spear. Mukisa frowned. She knew for a fact that Paul made it a habit of checking his weapons every night when they went back to the village, but perhaps he had been distracted last night. Very well. The entire village's next meal depended on what they and the rest of the hunters brought back, and she knew Paul wouldn't slack at his job.

He looked so content sitting there,

scraping away at the slate with his whetstone, and Mukisa felt this same contentedness spread through her as she watched. He had told her once, she remembered, that sharpening his weapons was calming to him. She had laughed at him — Paul was not one to find pleasure in violence, and it was common knowledge that the only reason he had become a hunter was because it meant he could find some spare time to himself. He would even risk the dangers of the forest for it. So to her, it was funny that he found it a soothing practice.

She saw Paul suddenly freeze in his place on the rock, and grimaced; perhaps he had heard her breathing. Not that it mattered — Mukisa was one of the few people by whom Paul didn't mind being interrupted. But she liked seeing him so relaxed, and now that moment was gone.

She silently crept forward, an idea sprouting in her mind, and unsheathed the knife at her belt, reaching him before he even turned around and holding the weapon mere inches from his head. He turned, and nearly ran his nose straight into the tip of the knife. Mukisa let out a peal of laughter as he gasped and fell backwards off the rock, startled.

Paul jumped to his feet, fuming. Mukisa poised the knife in her hand nonchalantly, a mischievous grin splayed across her face. She shoved the knife back into its holster and gave Paul a coy look.

"Damn it, Mukisa, I told you to stop doing that!" Paul sputtered, picking up the spear that he had tossed inadvertently on the forest floor.

She smirked. "You're a hunter. You're supposed to hear me coming. Nice job dropping your weapon at the slightest surprise, by the way—"

"I didn't want to hurt you," Paul grumbled, sitting back down on the rock. But it was a good-natured grumble. Mukisa laughed and leaned in, trying to steal a kiss, and he pulled back, a scowl on his face. But the scowl didn't last long — that slow smile of his crept right onto his face like it always did.

She continued the game. "Fine, mope. *I'm* going hunting," she said, starting to move away. "Feel free to join me, whenever you've tended to your pride."

"Come here," he said, reaching to pull her in, but she laughed, pulling away.

"I'm sorry, *you* just killed the mood. So…"

She sauntered away, and heard him jump up, chasing after her. They ran through the forest, laughing, their feet expertly finding their way through the brush. "Slow down!" he called out, "I want to show you something!"

Mukisa ran for another second, then abruptly stopped and turned to Paul, still laughing. He nearly ran into her — he had been preoccupied with getting something out of his pocket.

Mukisa suddenly realized what he was

11

holding and took a step back impulsively. It was a thin, threaded chain, with a bead in the center. It looked so meticulously made, the thin strips of leather woven together with such precision, the hole in the bead so painstakingly carved and threaded onto the chain.

Mukisa glanced up at Paul with wide eyes, her heart suddenly wreaking havoc in her chest. He seemed to be having his own little panic attack as well; his eyes nervously searched her face, begging for some sort of answer. She stared back down at the chain in shock, like it was a bomb, a fragile bomb, and she didn't know how to detonate it without blowing herself to bits.

"What… what is that?"

"I think you know what it is," he said breathlessly, and she knew it wasn't from the running.

Mukisa silently ordered her chest to maintain a steady rise and fall. He was right… she did know what it was. In fact, her mother used to have one of these. That didn't make it any less frightening that he was holding it out to her. Exhilarating, but frightening. "That's a wedding link, Paul."

"I know." His voice cracked, betraying him.

Her eyes flitted to his. "Paul, this isn't something to joke around with—"

"I'm not joking, Mukisa."

He looked so scared. Mukisa did a quick check, evaluating her reaction: perhaps her face was exhibiting the wrong emotions. She reached out and touched the bead gingerly. Not a bomb. Just a symbol of love and adoration. She smiled suddenly and lunged at Paul, hugging and kissing him as together they fell to the forest floor.

This was not at all what Mukisa had expected on such an average day, but she embraced the idea, taking in the warmth of his body as he returned her kiss, and the sound of his relieved laughter as she grabbed the link from his hands and fixed it around her head, the bead falling nicely onto her forehead.

That warmth stayed with her all throughout the day as they hunted; the spinning in her head didn't stop until they emerged from the woods with the other hunters, the carcasses of game slung over their shoulders, and hopped the fence surrounding the Southern Village. It stayed with her up until the moment that she realized that the village was unusually quiet, *unbearably* quiet; and the villagers greeting them when they arrived were not smiling, were only staring at her, saying, "I'm so sorry, child." The moment that she narrowed her eyes, saw her mother standing in the village green, and dropped her game before running to her.

2

The Others

Calam Carter always complained of back problems. He would constantly order his wife, Laila, to give him a good massage to relieve the pain. Failure to comply meant Laila would hide bruises for a week.

Adranna couldn't help but stare at her Papa's back. The knots fascinated her; they contorted the muscles just above his shoulder blades and made strange bulges in his skin, like burrowing gophers. She thought it looked as though extra limbs were about to sprout from the surface of his skin at any second.

One morning, as he was preparing breakfast for the family, he caught her trying to look at the knots. Quick and sharp his hand swung out and connected to her face, sending her back across the room. Adranna began to cry, holding her cheek and cowering as Papa stepped towards her, the breakfast forgotten. "Quit your starin', Adranna," he snarled, looming over her. He raised his hand again, a menacing threat to the tiny girl.

The door behind Adranna opened, and Mama came into the room, whisking her up in her arms. "How dare you touch my daughter," she breathed.

"She's my daughter, too," Papa sneered, taking a step closer. "Been my daughter since you made me be a father." Mama edged backwards, but the wall allowed Papa the upper hand. His gaunt face contorted into a devilish smile.

Suddenly there was a knock at the door. Papa frowned — he always hated being interrupted — and moved to answer it, allowing Adranna and her mother to breathe again.

It was Jezra, one of the village deputies, at the door. "Is everything all right?" she asked, poking her head inside. "I thought I heard a noise."

Papa laughed. "Oh, it was just Adranna runnin' around."

"She fell," Mama added feebly, and Adranna felt her mother's embrace tighten around her.

The answer was good enough for Jezra. She smiled. "Adranna, you know better than to run in the house. You could knock all the walls down!" And with a laugh, Jezra was off to patrol.

Papa closed the door and turned back to face his family, an angry look on his face. "You better stop makin' such a ruckus when we have a disagreement," he spat, moving closer to them. Mama

15

instinctively moved away from him, and he laughed. "What's wrong? Scared of me shovin' her around again?" The devilish smile returned to his face. "There are worse things I could do to her."

He would live up to this statement, as if it was something he was inclined to fulfill; and, after each offense, he would always whisper those words, and they would always be accompanied by his sneering grin.

◆

Chancellor Wallheart hurried to the courtyard in the center of the Western Village, pulling his waistcoat around his face to shield him from the rain that was beating down from the night sky. Several other men had had the same idea as he, finding shelter in the metal overhang. They sat around a table, passing around a jug, and talking rather rambunctiously amongst themselves. Chancellor guessed that the jug was almost empty by now.

John Weatherby pushed a chair out for Chancellor as he reached them. "Welcome, Sheriff," he exclaimed, handing him the jug.

Chancellor gave him a nod and took a swig of the ale inside. "Some good weather we're having, isn't it?"

They laughed. "It's Al's fault," one man said, "Wasn't he just sayin' yesterday that the dry weather was givin' him a headache, and wouldn't it just change it up a little?"

"Way to go, Al!" John cried, clumsily taking

back the jug.

Chancellor glanced around at the group. Most of the men, including John, were deputies, but there were a few diggers in their midst. He nudged the youngest of the group, no older than seventeen, in greeting: the freckle-faced boy had been quiet since his arrival. "Did you get all the shovels in the shed on time?"

The boy nodded exuberantly. "It wasn't even my shift, but I ran over to make sure they got everything in before the rain rusted it all out."

"You're a good man, Wyatt. You keep it that way." Chancellor turned to look out at the rain, but out of the corner of his eye he could see Wyatt blush a little, smiling.

"Yes sir."

John was going to town on that jug. Chancellor raised an eyebrow at him. "Take it easy, John, I don't want to have to take you in on your night off."

"I will be all sobered up by tomorrow morning, thank you," John said with a grin. Chancellor didn't doubt it... though John was no stranger to indulgence, he took his duties very seriously. He was arguably the best deputy on the team, maybe even better than Chancellor. He sometimes wondered how he had gotten asked to be Sheriff, instead of John, though he wasn't complaining. There was the old joke that Chancellor had been named with greatness in mind, though that particular greatness had never been achieved... but Chancellor begged to differ. He enjoyed his job as Sheriff, and he would argue with anyone that the title had more of a ring to it than any of the other titles in town.

A hush fell over the group of men, and Chancellor turned to see why. His heart dropped at the sight: standing before them was Marie Goodwin, a solemn look on her face.

Under any ordinary circumstance, it would be considered peculiar to see the Sheriff of one village crossing into another village's territory. That was just the politics of the matter, and Chancellor's comrades undoubtedly were thinking that very thought. But a lot more was going through Chancellor's mind. He and Marie shared a history — twenty years of history, to be exact. Though Chancellor had been unearthed in the Western Village, and considered it to be his home, he hadn't lived there all his life... about fifteen years had been spent in the Southern Village. It began with a decision to travel (and a heated argument about it with his father... travel was risky even in those days), and quickly escalated to a whirlwind of emotions, gentle kisses, late night escapes into the sheltered parts of the forest — and then, the birth of a beautiful baby girl. Marie hadn't let the job of motherhood interfere with her job as Sheriff; she had raised that baby right alongside her daily duties, and Chancellor would do what he could to keep up. The circumstances were such that in those days, a smile never really left Marie's face… something that did not quite remain true today, though truth be told that when it did appear, regardless of the separation, Chancellor had still never seen a more beautiful smile. They named the baby Mukisa, a nod to Marie's roots in the Northern Village, and Chancellor gladly accepted his new place of residence in the Southern Village, beside his beautiful new wife. Nearly twelve years later, the miracle of life heartily repeated itself: the two of them brought Cecilia into the world.

Then came the accident; and shortly after that, Chancellor's father fell ill, and he returned to the Western Village to care for him. In retrospect, it was probably more than a slap in the face to Marie that he remained after his father's death to take the position as Sheriff.

Chancellor stood slowly, and nodded to Marie. He wasn't quite sure how to act around her now… what did five years of distance really mean? "What brings you here, Sheriff?"

She stepped under the overhang, smoothing her dress of excess water, and returned his stare. "If I could have a word, Chancellor." He searched her eyes for any sort of clue as to her thoughts — annoyance? Sadness? Acceptance? Sometimes her ability to channel her true emotions into helpful emotions was infuriating — he couldn't get to the truth of what was really happening in her mind.

Chancellor narrowed his eyes. "Is this the time for a private conversation, Sheriff, or —?"

"*If I could have a word, Sheriff.*" Her gaze immediately turned icy. Perhaps it was unwise to test those waters just yet. He turned to the men around him. "Save some for me," he said, nodding to the jug. John held it up as a toast, and they all let out a little cheer.

He led her back out into the rain. "My cottage is just over there."

His cottage was only lightly decorated — a few reed tapestries made by local weavers broke the monotony of the walls, but the table and chairs were made of simple, unapologetic wood, void of fancy embellishment. Even after five years, Chancellor hadn't really gained any artifacts worthy of showing off. His reputation as Sheriff was as good as any conversation piece he could put in his sitting room, and he carried that with him. Of course, Marie still glanced around at the room with poorly masked envy, and Chancellor remembered what her quarters looked like: dry mud walls in stark contrast to the log cabin structure that Chancellor boasted, straw thatching instead of the tin roof that protected their heads at the moment. Though Chancellor wouldn't have minded straw thatching with this weather… it was certainly easier to talk over the pattering of rain on straw than it was with the clanging of water on tin.

Marie sat across from him, blankly staring

at the wall behind him. It vexed him a little: Marie had always been a woman of few words, but she usually managed to keep a civil conversation going. But her gaze had lost its coldness, and that was a step in the right direction.

"How's the village?" he prodded, breaking the awkward silence.

Marie's response was delayed, as if she couldn't quite find a way to articulate words. "The field's been acting strange," she said slowly.

"Oh? How so?"

"It's been a real struggle to unearth people from the mud."

"We all have our struggles, Marie."

Her eyes snapped up, and she stared at him for a long, unnerving moment. "The diggers have claimed that newcomers will virtually be sucked back under the mud, right before their eyes. Like someone's yanking them back down."

Chancellor raised an eyebrow. "All right, that's admittedly a little out of the ordinary. But that's life out on the field. Mayor Kenton was mentioning in his last visit that the other villages have been having some struggles as well."

That perked her interest. "In his last visit? When was that?"

Chancellor shrugged. "A few weeks ago."

She was visibly irked, and Chancellor steeled himself for the conversation that he'd had countless times before: why didn't he visit *us*, why is he talking to *you* and not *us*? While everyone would have loved for the Mayor to divide his time equally between the four villages, he of course spent most of his time in the Eastern Village, where he lived. And in the time that he was traveling between the villages, bringing provisions that the villagers wouldn't necessarily find in their own plot of land, he tended to favor the larger villages over the likes of the Southern Village… especially since it was the most remote of the Four Villages.

Chancellor could understand why the Southern Village could hold some resentment against the Western Village because of it, but he was tired of hearing about it. He knew that conditions weren't the best that they could be, and that for all intents and purposes, given their distance and their individual growth, the four villages should be separate towns, governed by separate mayors — but that was the way it was.

But much to Chancellor's surprise, Marie didn't complain. In fact, she remained silent. He searched her face suspiciously.

"How are the girls?" he asked. She raised her eyes to his face again, this time caught a little off guard. "Is… is Mukisa still terrorizing her peers?"

She still seemed a bit dazed, but a smile tugged at her lips. "Of course."

"And Cecilia? How is she?"

The smile faded from her face. She cleared her throat. "Something has happened, Chance."

Chancellor felt his insides go cold. "What?"

"Chance... Cecilia has fallen under."

He suddenly found himself standing, pacing, avoiding eye contact. Of course it would happen that as soon as life leveled out to a constant contentedness, his past would poke back into the picture and stir up trouble. But he would have much preferred it to be any other piece of news — *any* — than this. This, he wasn't sure how to handle.

Marie stood, unsure. "The boy she was digging up just—"

"Digging up? Why was she on the field at all? You *know* that she shouldn't be—"

"Chancellor." Marie's voice was firm, and it snapped Chancellor back to his senses. He stopped his pacing and stared at her pitifully, waiting for her to speak. "I didn't tell you this so that you could attack me. I told you this because you're her father, and you ought to know. Now, I will notify you as soon as she resurfaces—"

"Well, I'm going to help. I'll pay a visit to the Southern Village. You're always looking for more diggers, aren't you?"

"Chancellor. I think you should give yourself a proper mourning time—"

"She's not *dead*," Chancellor spat, and grabbed his coat, bursting through the door and out into the rain. He would go now... no matter that it was the middle of the night.

He heard Marie behind him, felt her hand on his arm. She twisted him to face her. "I know she's not dead," she said, gripping his arm fiercely. "But be realistic about this, Chance," she continued, almost at a whisper. "There is a possibility she won't come back."

Her own words seemed to affect her; Chancellor wondered if she had been suppressing the thought, preventing even herself from fully understanding it until at last she had to speak it out loud. She closed her eyes, trying to steady her breathing, and he tenderly reached up to push a wet strand of her hair back into place. But as soon as his fingers brushed her temple, her eyes flew open. She backed away uncomfortably, letting go of his arm and returning to her state of stony silence.

His hand fell to his side. "I'm not going to assume," he said unsteadily, "that she won't come back."

She nodded. "All right. Then let me go back first. To warn people of your arrival."

A feeling of unrest settled in Chancellor's chest. "The rest of the village doesn't care, do they?" he asked. "They're probably saying that it was only a matter of time, and she deserves to be under the field, aren't they?"

Marie sighed. "No, they—"

"They are. They're saying that everyone comes from the field, so it's only fair — how can you defend that?"

"Chancellor—"

"No, Marie, that's wrong, and you know it! Our child is stuck under the field, and you want to warn people that I'm coming to help get her out! As if she deserves the field, and not the open air—"

"*Chancellor*. I'm going to warn *Mukisa*."

He faltered. "Yes, of course." She eyed him momentarily with an exhausted countenance, then began to walk away. "Surely you're not going back in this weather?" he called out.

She gave him an annoyed glance over her shoulder. "Of course I'm going home. I have duties to attend to."

Chancellor nodded. Of course she did. She had her own life now. He watched her disappear into the night, and sighed. He could wait until morning.

◆

Mukisa sat up, heaving a sigh of frustration. She had been trying to sleep, but sleep just wasn't coming. It was too quiet here, now that there wasn't a small child sleeping in the corner of the room.

She stared at Cecilia's empty bed. If she kept her eyes closed long enough, she would begin to hear her, giggling in the corner. Of course it would happen that sleep — the one tactic Mukisa had to avoid thinking about her sister — would betray her and make her think about her all the more.

Mukisa had called an early night for herself, after her mother had announced she would be visiting the Western Village to break the news to Mukisa's father. She had warned Mukisa as she was leaving that he may want to come to the Southern Village for the mourning period, an idea by which Mukisa was greatly displeased. He could do his own mourning in his own village, she thought. He most certainly did not need to come here and disrupt things any more than they already were. But maybe Mama was wrong; maybe he would not return. Mukisa entertained that thought for a moment.

She wondered if her mother was back yet. Perhaps not... it was several miles to the Western Village, and she had only been gone for a few hours; Mukisa doubted that she would want to make the journey home in the dark. She had asked Mama Nina to take her shift at the Guest House, indicating that she would be gone til morning, but if Mukisa knew her mother, she didn't expect the conversation with her father to last more than a few minutes. Perhaps she would just want to get the trip over with and come back to her bed.

The only way to know for sure if she had returned was to check. Mukisa threw back her covers and jumped up, padding quietly to the door. The Guest House sat right next to her house, and was where her mother slept.

The Guest House served the purpose of

temporarily holding newcomers until permanent houses could be built for them, or until adopted families were found for them. Usually the latter, since most were unearthed when they were still young. During the day, the members of the village took shifts watching over the children, but it made sense that someone consistently take the night shift, and that someone was Marie. She had taken the night shift ever since she had moved to the village, making the Guest House essentially her home. Mukisa remembered the arguments between her parents, the constant back-and-forth between the Guest House and the family's home (which had been built next door for that very reason), but the arguments always had the same conclusion: she was right there if they needed her, and, as Marie was ever partial to her work, she could not bring herself to abandon her job of looking after the newcomers.

Upon their father's departure, Mukisa and Cecilia had remained in the family house, claiming it as their own while Mama continued with her night shifts. Mukisa liked to think their mother recognized that they were responsible enough to live there without her watchful eye; and yet, just as before, they were still close enough to her if they needed her. Of course, now that Mukisa was nineteen, it seemed perfectly suited that she have her own place, if she chose. Not all did — some preferred to continue living with their parents and care for them as they aged. That was what Paul was doing. A thought flickered through her mind: when she got married, would Paul move in here and leave his mama, or would they get their own place and leave Cecilia alone?

Cecilia. Cecilia was already alone.

Mukisa inched the door open quietly, and walked out into the night air. It was crisp and cool out, cool enough to mask the cold feeling that had come to rest in her stomach. A smattering of fireflies winked their lights in the darkness. She gazed at them, lost in thought, then drew her arms in close to retain heat as she peeked in through a window of the Guest House. It was a hopeless venture: she couldn't make much out in the darkness.

A moment later, she was standing outside another house, rapping on the wooden frame of the window to get the attention of the sleeper inside.

Paul drowsily picked up his head, and fumbled his way to the window. "What?" he asked in a harsh whisper.

"Come out," she whispered back. He sighed, rubbed at his face, and nodded.

She met him at the door. He lit a lantern, and the two of them began walking along the green. "I didn't wake your mama, did I?" she asked.

Paul shook his head. He wasn't awake enough yet for words. She slipped her hand around his, and he squeezed it. After a few moments, he asked, "How do you feel?"

"Cecilia's gone."

"Mmm." He glanced over at her. "For now."

She nodded. "They'll find her," she said in the most convincing tone she could muster. "Maybe it will take a while, but they'll dig her back up. They found Martin, didn't they?" Paul was silent, and Mukisa knew without even looking at him that he was trying to find the right words— truthful, but not too hopeless. She knew the reason for his hesitation, and answered her own question. "Of course, Martin was under the mud for almost thirty years."

She spoke of a man who had resurfaced from the mud about a month ago. She hadn't been alive when he had fallen under, but the day he resurfaced, it was as if the entire village let out a collective breath. That was always the case — they mourned an individual's fall, but there was always the unquestioned assumption that the villager would return — it was only a matter of time before the field would gift them back into the world. With Martin, it had taken a little longer than normal. Well... a lot longer than normal.

"But he was found," Paul stressed.

Mukisa bit her lip. "I could be almost fifty years old when she resurfaces."

"Or you could be a day older than you are now," Paul said, a small smile appearing

29

on his face.

Mukisa tried to return the smile, but could not. The cold feeling in the pit of her stomach was too strong. Instead, she watched her feet as they walked.

He squeezed her hand again. "If you want," he said slowly, "we can wait until she is found to be married."

Mukisa gave him a sharp glance. "Do you not want to—?"

"No! No, I do. But I know you want your family there for the occasion."

"But it could be *years*," she repeated.

Paul was silent for a moment. He shrugged. "So we'll wait. We'll still be together. We just won't have the celebration anytime soon."

"Or we could just get married now."

"Would you want that?"

Mukisa frowned. "No. I want my sister to be there. You're right."

They glanced up and saw Marie approaching from the edge of the forest. She looked a mess, her dark hair straying from her bun, her dress wrinkled. She looked up at the two of them, and nodded a greating. "He'll be coming," she said wearily, then made her way to the Guest House.

A heaviness settled in Mukisa's stomach. Paul glanced at her again. "How do you feel?" he asked, and this time Mukisa sensed a bit of trepidation in his voice.

She groaned and dropped his hand

abruptly. "I'm going to bed," she said, and stalked off before Paul could press her further.

3

The Mourning

The Southern Village prided itself in the great celebration that happened every month, setting off firecrackers, eating food, and enjoying one another's company. A large banner hung in the middle of the square, reading:

WE WELCOME OUR NEWCOMERS

Underneath the banner, the guests of honor were seated at a long, white clothed table, looking quite bewildered, as they had never participated in such a celebration — they would not fully appreciate their inauguration into the village until the next month, when they watched the fresh batch of newcomers with the same looks on their faces.

In one corner of the square, Mama Nina sat with a small group of children, holding their rapt attention with a story. The majority of the village respectfully gave the elderly woman the title "Mama", not because she was a mother (in fact, she had neither fostered nor born any children), but because of the wise way that she mentored each of the villagers as if they were her own. She had quite naturally fallen into the role of the village elder, quick as she was with wisdom and political insight, and always looking out for others' best interests. And she was the storyteller at every celebration — it was doubtful that even one villager had not sat by her feet at some point, enraptured, listening to her tell one of her tales. Sometimes, it was the tragic story of the young adventurers who wandered into the world beyond the Four Villages and became lost, never to be seen again; sometimes it was the tale of the First Man, the mysterious figure of legend who pulled the first newcomer from the fields so many ages ago. Sometimes, like tonight, she spoke the caricature of the field, turbulent and hot tempered.

"If you've ever taken a good look at the field," she began, "you'll notice that sometimes it moves of its own accord... like it's *alive*." A few of the children squealed. "And after all, it birthed each and every one of us, so you could say that it *is* alive. But just as it sends you off into the world, it will just as quickly call you back home for a visit. That's why we tell you young ones to stay off the field 'til we know you're ready... because sometimes the field gets jealous, and tries to take back its children. But we are loyal to the field, just like every other village is loyal to *their* field... if you give your creator the respect it deserves, it won't come after you..."

Her tale continued, peppered here and there by the gasps of the children, who glanced at each other with wild eyes, indoctrinated by their fear; and the adults would now breathe a little easier, knowing that they would from then on treat the field with caution.

From the throngs of celebration, Chancellor emerged, walking slowly past the various groups of celebrating individuals. He had originally planned on coming straight to the Southern Village that morning, but his mind had gotten the better of him, and he had wandered around in the forest for hours before even making it anywhere near his destination. It hadn't been the smartest decision, given the danger of the forest, but too much had been running through his mind: his daughter, gone; the rest of his family, waiting for his arrival. They had probably been worried about his whereabouts as he'd wandered the forest, arriving hours after he had promised.

Chancellor laughed to himself. Who was he kidding? His presence in the Southern Village, though requested, was certainly not wanted, and he could not even dream that Marie and Mukisa harbored any concern for his safety... that maybe some animal had gotten him along the way, or that he had tripped and broken his ankle... If anything, they were probably willing it to happen.

He tried not to look at the faces of the people that he passed. He knew that in the faces of the younger villagers, there would no doubt be fear, distrust... who is that? they would be thinking, and what is he doing in our village? But in the faces of the older ones, there would surely be some recognition... they would remember that he had once lived among them, had once joined in their celebrations as a part of their own village. But now they would only see him as the father of the fallen, and a stranger aside from that: Oh, the poor thing, running away at the first sign of trouble, only crawling back to mourn his daughter's fall. Maybe there would even be some hatred indicated in their glances, or a loathing sort of pity. Chancellor didn't particularly want anyone's pity at the moment.

So he avoided their stares, instead glancing down at the wild rose in his hands and twirling the stem thoughtfully in his fingers. Reaching the edge of the village square, he stopped. Here was a completely different scene: two women sitting amongst a sea of lit candles, a pile of roses at their feet, a circle of mourners surrounding them and supporting them.

Chancellor watched the two of them, his family, their heads down, candlelight reflecting the gloom on their faces, as all who were more than a few feet away danced and enjoyed the night. It was a preposterous practice the Southern Village had, he thought, mourning the fallen while celebrating the saved. It was meant to bring hope — hope that the fallen would resurface and be a part of next month's guests, to reinforce the idea that the field would always return its children — but to Chancellor, it just made the pain worse. The people of the Western Village had their separate ceremonies, as they should. There was a time for mourning, and there was a time for rejoicing... joining the two was just confusing, and insulting to the fallen. Barbaric, this was.

He approached them and placed his rose on top of the pile. Marie's eyes immediately found his, and he silently prayed that she was hiding relief behind that steady, emotionless mask that she invariably wore. He knew her well enough to know that he could exasperate some kind of emotional response out of her — perhaps he was the only one who had the ability to do this — but he was not about to make any such attempts on a night like this.

Mukisa, on the other hand, had no trouble showing her true emotions. She stood abruptly, boring a hole through Chancellor with the spite in her eyes. A young man stood and moved to Mukisa's side protectively, and Chancellor suddenly noticed the bead on her forehead. It was a startling realization that Mukisa might very well have a lover... so strange to think of his little girl as a grown woman. So strange to think of a man who could handle the wild woman that Mukisa could be.

"What is he doing here?" Mukisa said, her voice filled with poison. As if she didn't know.

To be honest, for a moment, Chancellor found himself asking the same thing. He remembered the day when the villages weren't nearly so hostile to each other — travel had not necessarily been encouraged, but at least tolerated. Now he was being verbally accosted by his own daughter.

He should have realized Mukisa would have a thing or two to say about his presence. But he would not let himself be pushed away so easily. "I have every right to be here," he said. "I'm her father."

"You really think she's ever called you that?"

The words stung; and he could not believe the audacity. He knew Mukisa would always have that uncontainable spunk in her... but have mercy, Marie could have taught her manners.

Marie reached out and touched Mukisa's arm. "Mukisa..."

Okay, so maybe she had tried.

Mukisa pulled away from her mother's

touch, storming away from them. The young man who had stood to support her began to move in her direction, but Marie stopped him and followed instead. She did not disappear, however, before sending an angry look in Chancellor's direction... perhaps he had exasperated her after all.

And just like that, it was as if Chancellor had stepped behind a veil. The celebration continued around him, and people brushed past him without so much as a glance... it seemed that, now that his presence had been acknowledged, the village was doing its best to pretend he wasn't here.

Chancellor escaped the noise of the celebration in the square and found himself standing at the edge of the field, staring out at its vastness. The darkness fell thick on him, and he couldn't help but remember the morbid phrase that one of his deputies had mentioned once: the mud of the sky. For that was what darkness was, wasn't it? Suffocating, numbing your senses... nothing was safe from it...

The field lay quiet before him, sleeping. Chancellor wished it would remain dormant forever. But that wouldn't do, either; then Cecilia would be trapped forever. Trapped forever in the talons of a sleeping beast. No matter how hard the villagers here reinforced the idea of "Mother Mud", that was all he could see the field as: a beast.

He tried to conjure up the picture of his daughter, her high-pitched squeal, her dark skin and bouncing curls. It pained him that it was so hard to hold the image in his mind's eye... but then, what he was remembering was not even what she looked like now. She'd had five years to grow and change, form her own thoughts and opinions, do what she liked. What kind of girl had fallen under the mud? The calm in the storm, like her mother? Or was she stubborn and fierce, like her sister? Had she been a happy child?

A rustling behind Chancellor made him start. He turned to see a tiny figure perched in a nearby tree, and his heart nearly jumped out of his throat — for a fleeting moment, he half expected it to be Cecilia. But no... pale skin, long waves of hair instead of tight curls...

The little girl stared at him with wide eyes. Perhaps he had found her hiding place, her thinking spot. He sighed. Yes, I've spoiled your fun, too, he thought. Why don't I just go home?

He glanced back at the field, and made one last resolve: not until she was found. He would not go home until Cecilia was found.

◆

The Southern Villagers often joked about how vastly different Marie's disposition was to her children's. Usually a child was matched to their adoptive family by personality, so as to give them a link, but Marie's children, in an inadvertent protest to the link derived from her very womb, had ended up just as rambunctious and outspoken — perhaps a little more like their father, at least in his youth — as Marie was calm and few-worded. It was not that she never had anything to say — she just withheld her right to judge people, and that left little else to be said.

But every once in a while, Cecilia or Mukisa (usually Mukisa) would get herself into trouble, and Marie would open up and give them her own private share of words — sometimes to rebuke but oftentimes to heal and to soothe, for the punishment was often in the consequences of the action.

Tonight, Marie saw that she would have to use words. Mukisa was alight with anger as she burst through the door to the Guest House, Marie following close behind. "He has no right to be here!" she cried, infuriated.

"Yes he does, Mukisa." Marie smoothed the folds of her dress. "This is a time of mourning, not of anger. I warned you that he was coming."

Mukisa whipped around to glare at Marie. Or no, she wasn't glaring *at* her — she was just glaring, and it happened to be her mother that she looked at. Marie was able to understand that, at least, about Mukisa — just because she had a lot of anger within her didn't mean that it was toward the person she was loosing it on. Marie could have given her all the warning in the world, but it still wouldn't help with the initial shock of seeing him. "He hasn't seen her in five years!" she seethed.

Marie smiled sadly, placing her hand on her daughter's cheek. It had both a startling and calming affect on her. "And he hasn't seen you in five years."

Mukisa stared into her mother's eyes, her anger having momentarily deflated. "Or you."

Marie smiled sadly, and patted Mukisa's cheek. It was true… it wasn't just his daughters that Chancellor had walked out on. When he'd left the Southern Village, she had thought, let him go where he wants to go… he'll return. And five years later, he had returned… but perhaps too late. And not with the intentions that she had originally hoped.

Not that she still laid claim to these hopes. Even thinking about having a husband back in her life exhausted Marie — she had changed a lot in five years. But that still didn't change the pain that his departure had brought in the first place. She glanced around the Guest House, trying to find something to distract her from this thought.

"The children will be back soon," she said. "Help me pick up."

"You're just changing the subject," Mukisa muttered. "He has no place here."

"Well, there's nothing we can do about that, now can we?" Marie turned back to her daughter, only to find that the room was now empty… Mukisa had already bolted out the door. She shook her head. My, but the child was good at running.

4

The Schism

The celebration bustled around Adranna and her Mama. Together they sat and watched Papa across the square, drinking and laughing with the other members of the Northern Village.

It was confusing to Adranna to see Papa fit in so seamlessly with these happy people, when just that morning he had tossed his mother across the room in the secret of their own home, filled with rage at a spilt bowl of porridge.

Mama blamed his animalistic behavior on the fact that he was still recuperating from the field. Papa had fallen back under when he was younger, and resurfaced just eight years ago... and people who had been under the mud for long periods of time *always seemed to have a hard time when they returned. A restless and mean-spirited attitude was normal, Mama said. It might take a long, long time to readjust back into normal life. Papa would eventually return to his kind, loving self.*

Adranna didn't think she believed that, though; he wasn't getting any closer to recovering. If anything, she could sense him decaying further and further. She hadn't known him before his fall, but from the stories Mama told her, he had been a much more pleasant person back then — the kind of person that Mama would marry, anyway. Mama probably thought she was marrying the same man when he came back out of the mud. But it was like something had been ignited when he was under the field; his readjustment was hampered by the fire that raged within him.

She didn't think Mama quite believed anymore that he was readjusting, either. Adranna caught a strange look of helpless awe on her face whenever Papa did something rash, as if she had expected him to be himself but was disappointed to find that he was instead an animal.

But as soon as he set foot outside of their house, he laughed and chatted with the other villagers and participated in games of catch and built homes with the other members of the building committee… he was a standup citizen, and no one would believe the dark things he did behind closed doors.

Papa was speaking to a visitor: the sheriff of the Southern Village, Lucas Clarke. Mama said the sheriffs of each village would occasionally visit each other, to give news or to share supplies when the mayor was too busy making his own rounds. The Northern and Southern Villages were the furthest apart of the four villages, but apparently Sheriff Clarke had some relatives in the Northern Village, so he deemed the visit worth it.

Adranna saw Papa point towards her and Mama, and the two men began to approach them. "Lucas, this is my wife, Laila, and my daughter, Adranna."

"What a pleasure to meet the two of you," the man said with a bright smile on his face. "Are you enjoying the celebration?"

"Of course," Mama smiled shyly, quickly reaching to play with Adranna's hair. It was a nervous habit; she was always skittish around new people.

"So am I," the sheriff replied, patting Papa's shoulder. "You've got yourself a lovely family, Calam."

"Thank you," he replied proudly, eyeing the two of them like they were a prize he'd won at the last round of Village Games. He reached out and pinched Adranna's cheek. "We got this one just a few months after we married."

Adranna pulled away from Papa, rubbing her cheek; but she made sure to flash the sheriff a smile to indicate she wasn't actually hurt by her father's hand. That lesson had been instilled in her years ago.

But Adranna's actions did little good. The sheriff suddenly gasped and reached toward Mama. "Oh! Are you all right?"

Mama recoiled instantly, but it was too late: he had revealed the large welt below her ear, fresh from that morning's tumble. "I'm fine," she said quickly. "I fell earlier today..." She glanced furtively at Papa, who had gone rigid at the mention.

"My wife," he chuckled, "always runnin' into things. Such a klutz."

Sheriff Clarke looked thoughtful for a moment before replying. "Oh, I know exactly the feeling," he assured Mama, smiling. "I often don't look where I'm going... I'm surprised I don't look like a polka dot pattern," he said, chuckling.

Sheriff Clarke's good-natured small talk was met with electric silence. Mama kept the polite smile etched across her face, and the man cleared his throat, nodding. "Well. It was very nice to meet you; I'll be over at the food table."

He strode away, leaving Mama to let out her sigh of relief and Papa to issue her a warning glare before following after the sheriff.

◆

Mama Nina stood before the small group of children, sizing them up for her next lesson. About three days a week she did this, with the older children, at least... the younger ones still pranced about on the green, enjoying their freedom, while their older playmates begrudgingly sat in wait of their philosophical exercise of the day. It was never a thoroughly thought out lesson, but would happen much like this: Mama would propose a thought, and the children would continue that thought until it had developed into possibly another thought, and another, and another. Mama had played Teacher for years now, and she never ceased to be amazed at the questions that the children asked when pushed toward the general vicinity of contemplation.

She smiled at them and began. "What sets us apart from the creatures in the forest?"

In the front of the group, a boy named Andrew raised his hand. "We live in the village."

Mama chuckled. "Correct, but I was hoping for a more in-depth observation. Dig a little deeper, Andrew. Why do we live in the village?"

He thought for a moment. "We made the village. And the other animals don't make anything."

"Birds make nests," a girl named Rosie piped up from the back row.

Mama smiled. "Yes, they do. Andrew?"

"Well, but they don't have tools."

"So what leads to tools?"

"Intelligence," an older boy, Billy, quipped.

"Okay. So we have become smart enough to reason that having baskets and knives and other tools might help us survive longer. Correct?"

Rosie sighed. "But birds wouldn't be able to use knives like we do. They don't have fingers like us."

"The specters have enough fingers like we do, but they don't use knives," Billy retorted.

"They've got claws. And they're stronger. They don't *need* knives as much."

"The specters aren't as smart as us," Andrew mumbled.

"What makes you say that?" Mama asked.

"We talk to each other, and they don't. We've got speech."

Mama raised a finger. "Does a hawk's call not communicate something to its neighbors? We may not know what, but we understand that the hawk speaks language. What do you think?"

"But that's exactly it… The specters are like the other animals in the forest," Billy jumped in. "They don't try to communicate with *us*. They don't seem to have any moral grounds, or care for more than the essentials of life. They are predatory."

Mama raised her eyebrows, surprised. "And what do you call what our hunters do in the forests?"

He smiled. "That's different. The hunters are providing their village with sustenance. The specters just… attack."

Mama frowned. She had not intended the conversation to steer so swiftly toward the specters. "What else makes us different?" she posed thoughtfully.

"Has a specter ever eaten one of us?"

Rosie asked, ignoring Mama Nina's attempt to shift the conversation.

"Not that I am aware of, no," Mama said slowly.

"So if they don't eat us, then why *do* they attack?"

"To make us fall under the field," Billy speculated.

"They do always seem to attack when the diggers are having an especially good week," Rosie giggled sardonically.

"That's just speculation," Mama said.

"So, what... they're some kind of guardians?" Billy asked. He smirked. "The field's lackeys?"

Mama sighed. "That makes the field sound a lot more terrible than it is—"

"Like a devil, swallowing up the souls it spits out." Rosie always had been poetic. Mama cleared her throat.

"The field births us," she reminded the children. "It doesn't spit us out."

"But why would it create something and then destroy it?" Rosie asked.

"It doesn't destroy, stupid," Billy scoffed. "It just takes you back, is all."

"That's right," Mama said, nodding, "you would simply be returning to your womb—"

"Well, it destroys a person's quality of life!" Rosie snapped back, glaring at Billy. "You go under, you don't remember anything. And that isn't really living, is it?"

There was a silence for a moment. Mama

Nina's heart ached for Rosie. Her mother had fallen under the mud while digging a few months ago, and had yet to be returned to the village.

"So you believe we come from a thing that doesn't want us to live?" Mama prodded gently. "Is that what you think, Rosie? Then why create us in the first place?"

The children glanced at one another, unsure. Rosie looked back up at Mama, and this time her mouth opened timidly, wavering before responding. "Because it's evil."

The answer took Mama by surprise. "Creating life is evil?"

"No, but creating life and then snuffing it out for no reason is. Isn't it? It's just a power play. So the field must be evil."

"Interesting." Mama thought for a moment. "But what makes you think there's no reason?"

"What, are you asking if we're good enough to deserve a chance to live?"

"Is that the only reason the field would want to swallow us back up? If we're not good enough?"

"But we've got plenty of good going for us," Rosie muttered. "We've created moral systems, ways of keeping the peace... And we're intelligent! Far more intelligent than the animals in the forest or the specters in the sky..."

"Yet we still fall under the mud."

"It's not fair!" Rosie said tearfully. "It's

not fair that good people have to fall under, while bad people still stay on top..." She looked away suddenly, past the group of children, tears still dribbling down her cheeks.

Mama Nina's brow furrowed. She followed Rosie's distracted gaze; her attention had been caught by the group of hunters who was gathering, about to head into the forest. Mukisa was among them.

Mama Nina turned back to Rosie, who still watched Mukisa with a look of trepidation in her eyes.

Mama frowned. "You don't believe that, do you?" Rosie quickly snapped out of her daze, and her eyes widened. Mama sighed. "Children, I will discuss with you all day the purpose of our life and origins, but I will not tolerate any insinuations that there are people who have less capacity for good than others. You all have the potential to do good, and you all have the potential to do bad. Sometimes we choose to do things that turn out to be not so good. Or sometimes it isn't even a matter of choice; it simply happens. But that doesn't mean we can't learn from those mistakes. I want you to keep that in mind in your interactions with others."

Billy cleared his throat. "But what if people keep making mistakes? If we have just as much potential for good as we do bad, then there will be those who continue to choose to do bad. When do we make the decision to stop making them learn from their mistakes, and just stop them altogether?"

Mama Nina smiled. This was a good topic to turn to. It was safe — she knew how to monitor it. She loved it when the children led the discussion, but she loved it even more when it was a discussion with which she felt comfortable. "What a good question. Does anyone have any thoughts?"

♦

Mukisa's knife found the boar's heart with perfect accuracy, instantly killing the beast: the merciful route. No pain for the village's dinner.

She jumped down from her perch in the tree she had been waiting in and took back her knife. Grabbing the boar's hindquarters, she dragged it slowly through the brush and returned to the day's hunting base, where Martin, their newest hunter, waited, guarding the game that the rest had caught already.

She rolled the animal's corpse carelessly onto the pile. "How goes it, Martin?"

The sullen man barely lifted his hand in reply. He was angry that he was stuck as guard. But truth be told, he was not a very good hunter — his small stature made it difficult to keep up with the rest of the hunting party. In fact, he hadn't been much good at any of the jobs he had tried since resurfacing from the field. Mama Nina said that it was because

he had lost so much of his life to the mud...
anything that had been agreeable within him
had been sucked out of him, leaving him a
gaunt, snarky middle-aged man with only a
few years of memory, and an awfully big chip
on his shoulder about the whole matter. The
village had tried to involve him in many
different jobs, and hunting just happened to be
next on the list for him... but so far, he had not
found his niche. The hunting party was
content to just stick him as the guard until he
gave up and moved on to the next job.

Mukisa smiled inwardly — she couldn't
even remember the last time she was chosen
to be guard. Her hunting skills were too
valuable.

"Where's the water?"

"Over there." He gestured towards a
large, sun-cracked jug, about halfway empty
by now. Mukisa tipped the jug and caught
some of the water in her hands, slurping it up
thirstily.

Turning, she saw Martin staring curiously
at her. "What?" she demanded.

"Sorry," he mumbled, his face going red.
"I was just... you look ridiculous with that
thing on your head."

Mukisa's hand instinctively rose to the
bead on her forehead. She kept forgetting it
was even there... but when she was reminded
of it, it felt heavy and constricting. Ever
since Paul had suggested the other night that
they wait until Cecilia was found before

starting any preparations for the wedding, Mukisa had been trying to decide whether that was such a practical idea… if they waited, it really could take years. But when had Mukisa ever made a practical decision simply because it was practical? No, it felt right to wait. She needed to have her whole family there. It was the only time she felt whole herself.

Well… her whole family, meaning her, her Mama, and Cecilia, and of course, the addition of Paul and his mother. She had spent the last five years reinventing the word "family" into more than just those she cared for — it was also about those who cared for her. And now… *he* was pushing his way back into the picture, just to mess everything up. She squirmed uncomfortably. It wasn't fair! It wasn't even like he was going to stick around, he would just be disrupting things and then leaving everyone to pick up the pieces yet again. Just because he was her father did not mean that he deserved to be a part of her family. No, he would have no part in her wedding.

But that still left the question of how long they would wait.

She lifted her chin defiantly at Martin's comment. "Would you be saying the same if someone gave it to you?"

Mukisa winked sardonically, and Martin gave a grumble.

Just then Paul appeared at the edge of the clearing, a concerned look on his face.

"We've got trouble," he said simply, before disappearing back into the thick of the trees. Mukisa narrowed her eyes and stalked after him. She shook her head at Martin, who had begun to rise. "Stay right where you are and do your job, Jewelry Boy."

Martin rolled his eyes. "Yes, this is clearly the job for me," he remarked snidely before sitting back down.

Mukisa quickly caught up with Paul; he motioned for her to be quiet, and they positioned themselves behind a large rock, peering down the slope at the sporadic splay of trees and underbrush.

From where they were hiding, they could see two men walking starkly through the woods. They were clearly not hunters — if they noticed Mukisa and Paul, they completely ignored them, and tromped through the underbrush loudly enough for anyone to hear. The younger of the two, tall and lanky with accentuated freckles and a head full of coppery hair, stopped and looked around.

"John, how close do you think we are?" he asked.

The one clearly named John, lean and well built with an authoritative air, stopped beside him and pointed off into the woods. "It should just be a mile up that way," he mused. Mukisa exchanged a nervous glance with Paul... that was the direction of the village.

The younger boy sighed, his shoulders slumping forward. "It just seems so far."

"Come on, Wyatt. The sooner we get there, the sooner we can find her, and the sooner we can go home."

They continued walking, and Mukisa narrowed her eyes. Her? Who was *her*? Well, she wasn't going to let them *find* any of her people, not if she could help it. She scrambled down the hill, still masked by the trees, getting closer to the strangers.

Paul hissed at her from behind. "Where are you going? They could be armed!"

She turned to give him a deprecating glance. "Paul, they're talking about someone from our village. I don't know what they have in mind, but I don't intend to let them go through with it. And besides... so what if they're armed?" She held up her knife, letting it glint proudly in the sunlight. "So am I."

She flashed him a grin and crept further down the hill, peering at her prey through the brush. She could hear Paul following behind her... not loud enough to draw attention, of course, though she doubted the half-wits would even notice.

The strangers were now only a few yards away, and walking straight towards them. Suddenly John held out his hand, stopping Wyatt.

"Stop. Something's not right."

Wyatt's eyes got wide. "What do you mean?"

"I don't know, just something doesn't feel—"

Mukisa rolled her eyes and stepped out from the bushes, quickly grabbing hold of Wyatt and positioning her knife at his throat. "Look, I've found two idiots, crossing into our hunting territory. How convenient."

John's face reflected the appropriate amount of surprise and fear that Mukisa was hoping for, and the squeal from the ginger boy within her grasp had the same satisfying effect. Behind her, Paul bounded up, spear firmly gripped in his hand.

"We didn't know—" John began shakily, holding up his hands. "We come in peace. We're from the Western Village—"

Mukisa regarded him coolly. "Then I can hardly believe you come in peace."

"Let him go, Mukisa," Paul said, quietly but firmly.

She glanced at him, annoyed. "No way," she muttered. She stared John down. "You two are in our space, walking around here talking about going after someone from our village. If kidnapping's on your mind, then hunting's on mine." She smiled sweetly.

Wyatt squirmed beneath her blade. "I really think there's been a serious mis-understanding—"

"We're not here to kidnap anyone!" John said quickly. "Our sheriff came to your village to find his daughter. We're just here to get him back."

A wave of disappointment washed through Mukisa. She snorted. "Then take him," she replied. "We don't want him."

"They're just here for Chancellor," Paul said slowly. "…And he won't leave until Cecilia is found. Kis, they're offering to help."

Mukisa sighed and let go of Wyatt. He dropped to the ground like a sack, stumbling back towards John and hiding behind him. Mukisa pointed her knife at them, waving it for emphasis. "All right. You'll come with us to the village. And as soon as your business is done there, you will leave and take your sheriff with you. But if you even make the slightest move to hurt one of our people, I will take the liberty of cutting the both of you into little pieces—"

"Mukisa!" Paul cut in sharply.

Mukisa cleared her throat. "All right, all right." She dropped her knife to her side, hoping that the strangers would take it as a welcoming gesture. "Follow me."

♦

Marie stood at the edge of the field, staring calmly out at the diggers, hard at work. Chancellor was among them… apparently he had been on the field even before the sun had peeked over the horizon and people had begun to trickle from their homes. The other villagers had not been too thrilled with his presence. Marie had all but needed to restrain Mukisa as she and the rest of the hunters had made their way past the field to go into the forest. She had a feeling she'd have to keep an eye on her daughter right up until the moment that Chancellor left.

She smoothed the folds of her dress, and cleared her throat. "Chancellor!"

Chancellor looked up from his position on the field, wiping his brow and inadvertently adding more mud to it.

Marie smiled. "Take a break." She turned and walked over to the Guest House, not even glancing back to see if he would follow. She knew that he would.

And sure enough, just moments later, as Marie folded clothing that had been brought in for the newcomers, Chancellor poked his head through the door. He glanced around at the few sleeping children, and Marie nodded to him. "Come in."

He timidly entered, trying to be quiet. "So you're still staying at the Guest House, then."

"Did you think I would abandon the children?"

"No… I just figured you would move in next door."

Marie smiled. "The girls do just fine without me. And I'm close enough to help when they need me."

"You never worried about them causing trouble?"

Marie tried to subdue the anger that suddenly swelled in her. Here he was, trying to resume his fatherly role after being back for less than a day. She took a pause before answering. "They may be a handful, but they are responsible. And besides, Mukisa is an adult now. She is soon to be married, if you haven't noticed."

Chancellor nodded. "Yes, I saw the bead. Is it the boy who was with her last night?"

"Yes. His name is Paul."

"I'll have to get acquainted with him."

"I don't know if that's such a good idea, Chance. She doesn't exactly favor you at the moment."

Chancellor sat on the edge of an empty bed, sighing. "What am I supposed to do then?"

"Well, you can start by trying to make up for the past five years, if that's possible. And *then* you can work on fitting yourself into her life."

"That isn't possible. Not in the next few days."

"Well, Chance… that is the sacrifice you made when you chose to live in the Western Village."

Chancellor stood instinctively, seething. *"It's my home."*

Marie dropped an article on the pile of folded clothing in front of him and stared at him calmly. "And the North was mine."

Chancellor glared at her, not sure of how to respond. She just smiled quietly, and picked up another wrinkled article of clothing.

"Did you call me over just to rile me up?"

"No. I also want to confiscate your

baton."

He gave her a withering look. "Anything that *isn't* meant to rile me up."

Marie held out her hand, waiting. "I'm not trying to. These are just the rules, plain and simple. You hold no jurisdiction in the Southern Village; there is no need for you to carry a weapon with you."

Grumbling, Chancellor unfastened his baton from his belt and dropped it into the palm of her hand. She calmly put it beside her and continued folding.

"I also wanted to know where you slept last night."

Chancellor blinked. He hadn't slept. The villagers had all retired to their beds, and he had snuck back onto the field and dug through the night. Not the smartest idea, given that the chance of falling under was always more likely at night, but there it was… he wouldn't be able to sleep anyway, so he might as well not try.

"I don't need anybody to host me, if that's what you're aiming at," he said politely.

"Well, we can't have you sleeping out in the cold, just you and the specters. I'm sure Anthony would host you if you asked."

Anthony had been a close friend of Chancellor's before he had moved back to the Western Village. He was one of the older hunters, and probably could have retired if he felt like it, but he liked being involved. Alas, though Chancellor had seen him since coming to the Southern

Village, he hadn't spoken to him. Frankly, Anthony hadn't given him the opportunity to speak to him. Chancellor supposed that, much like the others in the village, he had not taken his departure well. Whatever friendship they once had was nonexistent now, and truth be told, Chancellor couldn't blame Anthony for ignoring him.

"I'm fine. I don't want to stir up any more animosity between the villages, as it is."

A cry came from one of the occupied beds, and a little girl sat up, eyes wild. Chancellor breathed a sigh of relief at the distraction. Marie acted quickly, rushing to the girl's side. "Shhh, it's okay. It was just a nightmare."

The girl slumped back down in bed, breathing heavily. Marie rubbed her back soothingly.

Chancellor recognized the girl. "I saw that girl in a tree last night." The girl fixed her gaze on Chancellor, her eyes not yet completely drained of their crazy.

"This is Catherine," Marie said. "She was unearthed two weeks ago, isn't that right, Catherine?"

Catherine looked up at Marie, finally calming down. She closed her eyes and almost immediately fell asleep, exhausted. Marie stroked her hair lovingly before standing. She led Chancellor to the door, and they stepped outside, Marie closing the door carefully behind her. "That's happening again."

"What, the nightmares?"

Marie nodded. "It seems a child doesn't come across this threshold lately without having at least one nightmare while they're here. I miss the old days, when they woke up with smiles on their faces."

Chancellor watched her stare dolefully at the field for a moment, lost in thought. She was still beautiful, even with her hair pinned up in a hurry, an inky heap perched atop a bronze complexion. Beautiful and yet carrying so much sadness. "Marie... I won't leave until we get her back."

Marie turned to look at him. If it was possible, his words had made her look even more sad. "There you go, using the word 'we' again."

Suddenly a commotion near the square caught their attention, and Chancellor did a double take: Mukisa and Paul walked into the square, pushing John and Wyatt along. What were they doing here? A crowd of villagers formed to see what the commotion was, and Chancellor and Marie exchanged looks, hurrying over to them.

John saw Chancellor as they approached, and a look of relief crossed his face. "Chancellor, am I glad to see you!"

"What's going on?"

"The Western Village needs their sheriff back," John said, locking eyes with Chancellor and giving him a meaningful look. "And I know him too well... He's not coming back until he makes sure things are all right for his kin. Figured we could help speed up the process."

Mukisa butted in. "They were trespassing in our neck of the woods," she stated plainly.

"This probably isn't the best time to mention this," Wyatt cut in, "but it's not really *your* neck of the woods, no one really *owns* it—" Mukisa glared at him, and Wyatt quickly turned his gaze to the ground.

"Mukisa, why don't you and Paul go back to the woods to hunt?" Marie said calmly.

"No way!" Mukisa objected. "I don't trust them. They could be here to push people back under the mud for all we know—"

"*Why* would we do that?" Wyatt protested.

Marie frowned at her daughter and turned pointedly to Paul. "Paul, why don't you and Mukisa go back to the woods to hunt?"

Paul glanced at Mukisa and nodded, grabbing her arm gently. She rolled her eyes and stepped away from the group, though not before roughly pulling her arm away from Paul in defiance.

John stepped forward. "Sheriff Goodwin, my name is John Weatherby, and this here is Wyatt Pine. We are from the Western Village, and we are here to help you dig. For as long as it takes to find your — and our own sheriff's — daughter."

It was the quickest of glances that Marie gave to Chancellor, but he knew exactly what she was thinking: how much more unwanted excitement are you going to bring to my village before you go home?

Marie turned back to John. "Well, it's really not my decision," she replied. "That's up to the people." She turned to the crowd of onlookers. "All right, everyone, let's pull out the benches… we're having a town meeting."

♦

The villagers worked together to pull the long wooden benches that were stationed throughout the village onto the square. Just about everyone fit on the benches, but today they weren't ready to sit… they stood in throngs, talking angrily amongst themselves and shooting dirty looks at Chancellor, John, and Wyatt, who sat off to the side.

Mukisa watched her mother as she stood at the front of the assembly and held her hands up. She was trying to quiet the crowd, a task which was well beyond her ability at this moment in time; Mukisa considered helping her, but she found herself too exasperated that the meeting was even taking place to begin with. Instead she sat sullenly in her seat (at least she was cooperating in that aspect), her eyes drilling a hole into the bench in front of her. Paul sat silently beside her, an apprehensive look on his face.

It took several minutes to get everyone seated and quiet. Finally, Marie cleared her throat. "As most of you have probably heard by now, we have some visitors from the Western Village," she began. "I know this is out of the ordinary, but if you could please try to make them feel welcome while they're here—"

"Why *are* they here?" a voice called out from the crowd.

Marie glanced at Mukisa, a hesitant look on her face. Mukisa was sure she was working in her head to properly convey the meaning of the Western Villagers' visit without adding to her own family's torment — no need to inform those who hadn't already made the connection that their family had once again drawn foreigners to town. Besides, who would be happy that there were foreigners in town because a bastard had fallen under?

Marie's words were as vague as possible. "They're here to help with the digging for a while."

Another villager stood. "We don't need any help!"

A cheer rose up from the benches, and Mukisa felt a warmth spread through her chest. Never had she been more willing to back a statement made by the masses.

"How long are they gonna be here?"

Marie frowned. "I don't know the answer to that. But we need to show them hospitality while they're here. You would want them to do the same thing if you were visiting their village."

Mukisa heard a sharp laugh from the outskirts of the assembly, and turned to see Martin, his squat, pale frame leaning lazily up against a tree. "I wouldn't be caught dead visiting their village!"

Laughter went up throughout the entire assembly. Mukisa caught a glimpse of the Western Villagers shifting uncomfortably in their seats.

"First things first," Marie said, raising her hands for quiet again, "we need to decide whether they'll actually be helping us dig."

John stood on the spot, regarding the villagers indignantly. "Of course we're helping! We came all this way —"

"Sit," Chancellor said, reaching out from his place on the bench and placing his hand on John's shoulder, "and let the people decide what will happen in their own village."

Upon having given his warning, he looked up and caught Mukisa's eye. She quickly turned back to her mother, trying to ignore the surge of anger that shot through her at his glance. It was all she could do not to throw something at the man. Her mind buzzed, retreating from the presence of the crowd momentarily and blotting out the noise of the assembly. She could hear the dull thudding of her heart. She remembered a trick that Mama Nina had taught the children years ago: *Child of the field, child of the field*, she murmured to herself, then as quickly as she had tried, gave up. There was no use; the mantra was supposed to remind her that they all came from the same place, but Mukisa had never had much luck with that sentiment, given that she could not say the same about herself.

Beside her, Paul's elbow brushed up against her own, and she instead focused on his touch to distract her from the absurdity of the meeting; and then she was back, and the assembly came in crisp and clear once again.

Her mother was surveying the crowd shrewdly. "Any opinions?"

Murmurs ran throughout the crowd.

With this sudden resurge of clarity, Mukisa shot up from her seat. "No!" she cried. The crowd turned to face her, caught off guard. "We don't," she continued, looking directly at her father as she spoke the words, "need anybody's help. And we shouldn't trust them, just because they come in with their hands up."

"Now wait just a second," Mama Nina spoke up from the crowd, slowly and creakily pushing herself up to a standing position. "We need all the help we can get. I say, whether we think we can trust them or not, we should accept help when we are offered it."

Mukisa's confidence withered at the old woman's words. She realized in dismay that most of the responses, though still in a grumbling fashion, were in agreement with Mama Nina.

"All right, then," Marie announced. "They'll dig."

Mukisa sat back down, fuming.

"Second line of business," Marie continued, "these folks need a place to stay. Do we have any volunteers to host a guest?"

It was suddenly remarkably easy to hear the crickets singing in the forest.

"Come on, folks. We need three households, whether you like it or not. It's either volunteer, or we'll assign you somebody."

Still silence.

Marie glanced around at the stony faces of the crowd, and shook her head. She pointed. "The Gardeners. You will host a visitor."

Mukisa craned her neck to see the entire Gardener family complain loudly, sending the entire assembly into chaos once more.

"Why can't they just stay at the Guest House?!"

"They ain't stayin' with the children!"

"People! People, settle down—"

From the hubbub, Mukisa saw Wyatt stand and stride to the front of the assembly. "What is wrong with you people?!" he cried.

The crowd went dead silent. Wyatt hesitated, and a look of dreadful realization crossed his face as the attention of the mob of angry people turned to him. Mukisa heard a faint hissing, and realized it was John, motioning urgently for Wyatt to return to his seat.

Wyatt cleared his throat, nervously glancing around. "Look… look, we're no different than you. We're not here to hurt you, we're not here to steal from you… we're here to help you." He began to gain confidence as the assembly avoided eye contact. "I'm not saying you have to be happy about it, but you could at least hide your disdain."

With that, he nodded assuredly, somewhat proud of his little speech, and went back to his seat.

Silence blanketed the assembly again; but it was a different silence… still no one wanted to volunteer, but there was now an undertone of shame.

"I volunteer to host a visitor."

Mukisa choked on a sharp intake of breath. The crowd around her searched in their midst for the sound of the voice, but she didn't have to look very far: the words came from beside her. Paul stood, ignoring her shocked stare.

"I volunteer to host one of the visitors in my house," Paul said with a kind of timid certainty. He glanced at his mother, who sat on the other side of him. "With your consent, that is, Mama." The woman heaved a sigh, avoiding eye contact, but nodded.

At the front of the assembly, Marie smiled. "Thank you, Paul. Anyone else?"

As the assembly exchanged guilty looks, Mukisa saw Paul sneaking a look at her.

She quickly averted her gaze, holding her chin up and focusing all her attention on her mother, and heard his quiet sigh next to her.

After a moment, the Peterson family volunteered.

"And one more."

From the back, Anthony stood, raising a weathered hand. He glanced over at Chancellor, who gave him an appreciative nod.

With the meeting finally adjourned, the villagers broke apart and despondently trickled into their homes.

Paul stood, reaching for Mukisa to kiss her goodnight, but she pulled away coldly; no doubt she wouldn't speak to him until tomorrow because of his decision. Fine. Two could play at that game. He put his arm around his mama and, motioning for Wyatt to follow, began the slow walk home.

Paul opened the door to their modest home and helped his mother inside. Behind them, Wyatt gingerly stepped into the doorframe, not sure whether to enter the room just yet.

"Good night, Mama," Paul said, kissing the old woman on the forehead. She smiled and patted him on the shoulder. Then she turned to Wyatt, becoming very somber and nodding to him before leaving the room.

Man and boy stood there staring at each other for a moment. Paul cleared his throat. "She can be pretty stubborn. But you're welcome here."

"Thanks," Wyatt replied weakly, finally stepping into the hut.

Paul gave a sheepish smile. "Well, uh, we don't have any extra beds, but I can give you a couple blankets…" He began to sort through a wooden chest in the corner of the room.

"That's fine. I don't need a lot."

Paul pulled out some blankets and tossed them to Wyatt. Wyatt spread them out over the cold floor, situating himself. He glanced at Paul, who was still awkwardly watching him, a look on his face that clearly stated he had something to say. Wyatt humbly waited.

It took him another moment to find words. "Hey…" he began, then looked as if he had changed his mind, then shook his head and continued. "I think it's great, that you all came out to help. The girl who fell under is, uh, is my betrothed's sister. So…" He glanced off at a corner of the room bashfully. "I think it's really great."

Wyatt smiled at him, but there was a piece of guilt nagging at him. The truth of the matter was, they were less there to help, and more there to reclaim what was theirs. If helping happened while they were at it, then so be it. "We just want our sheriff back."

Paul nodded understandingly. He politely smiled and left Wyatt to get comfortable on the floor.

A few huts down, Chancellor sat quietly in a chair facing Anthony. Anthony's husband, Joshua, had excused himself to the bedroom, being able to recognize when two old friends needed to talk, but so far, neither of them had said a word.

Chancellor broke the silence. "Thank you for volunteering."

Anthony shrugged. "Someone had to do it. And I thought, anyone else would probably not have the decency to mince their words."

"What do you mean?"

"About Cecilia." Anthony's eyes reflected surprise. "What, do you honestly think another household would leave you in peace?"

"Look, I realize it's been a while since I've been here—"

"I didn't mean that," Anthony replied slowly. "I… what I mean is… I'm not about to start the conversation that everyone else would start with. The blessing of falling back under, the thought that it might do her good, and all that…"

"Birdshit."

Anthony eyed him thoughtfully. "Like I said. I'm not about to have that conversation with you." He cleared his throat. "So I expect I won't be seeing too much of you."

Chancellor glanced up, surprised. "Is that so?"

"You were out digging last night, weren't you?" he asked, and Chancellor hesitantly nodded. "Well, I expect you'll want to keep at it."

Chancellor slowly smiled, the realization of what Anthony was saying sinking in.

"Thank you. Thank you for letting me stay in your home, Anthony."

Anthony held up a hand. "This isn't to say we're on friendly terms again," he said. "You've still got some grievances to make up for. As you said yourself, it's been a while since you graced us with your presence. Leaving your family was not a wise decision, not in my book. And you left more than just your family behind."

Chancellor studied the pained look on Anthony's face, and nodded gravely. "I realize that. And I'm not going to promise that I'll be able to make up for it. But I will try."

Anthony sighed. "Well, go on, then," he said, waving him toward the door. Chancellor quickly removed himself from the hut, heading for the field.

5

The Hunger

Martin wasn't even focusing on the field — his vision just kept on sliding in and out, like the tides of a sea. What was holding his attention was the noise of the field, the squelching sound the mud made as it rolled about of its own accord, stretching its muscles on its daily exercise routine. The sound of it pulled on him, intoxicating him… he hadn't yet tried his hand at digging, but he was sure that he would have felt at home amidst these sounds.

But he would have to wait. The one job that people said was the most rewarding, which connected you with your origins and deepened your sense of place, was the last on the list of jobs that Martin had been tearing through. It seemed to him like that maybe meant it wasn't all that spiritually fulfilling, if the village left it as a last resort.

Martin dreaded reaching the end of that list. Despite the strange allure that the field seemed to have, he knew that the end of that list meant that Martin still hadn't found his place.

An awful feeling wrenched through his body, one that he could not entirely place his finger on. Maybe it was self-hatred... whatever his life had been like before this, it was over now. He felt like a lump of nothing.

A group of children bumped into him as they passed, knocking him back to his senses. A knot of pain clenched the muscles in his shoulders, and he reached up to rub them. He glanced at the door to the Guest House, where he had been assigned for the next few days — so said Marie Goodwin, Village Dictator — and frowned. Fantastic... just what he needed, a bunch of sniveling children to put him in a good mood. He could not wait to fail at this job.

Mama Nina approached him from the other side of the village green, carrying a basket of fruit. "Are you ready?" she asked with a smile.

"I reckon I'll have to be," Martin said bluntly, following her into the Guest House. The children were still asleep; they always overslept, the lazies.

Mama Nina put down the basket of fruit, seated herself, and pulled a basin full of clothing toward her, patting the chair next to her. "Come," she whispered, "help me fold."

Martin scoffed. "I'm not folding laundry," he muttered.

Mama Nina's look of surprise was minor; taking the situation in stride, she nodded to the basket of fruit. "Then you can distribute a piece of fruit to the bedside of every sleeping child, for their breakfast."

"That sounds like the most fantastic use of my time," Martin replied snidely.

She smiled, not to be moved. "You can either pass out the fruit, or you can help me fold. I've given you a choice."

Martin stared moodily at the fruit and muttered to himself. Mama returned to her folding.

Martin took a piece of fruit out of the basket and plopped it dully at the bedside of one of the sleeping children. He turned to look at Mama Nina. He plodded to the next bed, and plopped another fruit down. He turned to look at Mama Nina.

Mama folded the article of clothing in her hands, placed it on her lap, and leaned forward, hands clasped. The way she studied him, as if he were an oddity, made him uncomfortable. "Martin," she said slowly, "is there anything I can do to ease your readjustment into the village?"

Martin glared at her. "I think I've

readjusted just fine, thank you." Mama smiled at this. He tried to make his glare more menacing. "Quit smilin', would you?"

Mama chuckled. "I'm sorry. I didn't realize that affected you so negatively. I'll try to throw in some neutral facial expressions every once in a while." She continued folding. "But it seems to me that you do feel out of sorts here. Like you don't quite belong yet."

"I was under the damn mud for thirty years," Martin snapped, slumping into a nearby chair. "You could give me a minute."

Her smile became sad. "I'm just trying to get you back to your old self."

"My old self is gone, lady. There ain't no goin' back to the kid I used to be."

"I don't mean your old self, the child. I meant…" She looked as if she was about to say something, but changed her mind. "It's clear you've changed. I'm just worried about what's behind that change." She shrugged. "Everyone keeps saying that maybe you just haven't found your niche yet."

"I don't need no niche," Martin said with a scowl.

"*I* think your niche is to find the worst in every situation."

Martin gave her a sour look. "And your niche is to say mean things to unpleasant people, is it?"

Mama raised an eyebrow. "I only speak the truth. Not my fault you made the truth into what it was."

Martin stood roughly and put down the basket, about ready to leave, when the door creaked open and Wyatt appeared at the door. "Hello," he said uncertainly, entering quietly. "Um... I was told there might be an extra cot here?"

Mama Nina nodded. "Do you need it?"

"Yes." He swallowed. "Well... I need to move it to one of the cottages. I was told—"

"Of course. Not everyone has an extra bed in their home, and I'm sure you'd rather not sleep in a room of twenty."

Wyatt sheepishly glanced around at the sleeping children.

Mama prodded Martin forward. "Martin, will you help this gentleman carry a cot to his new quarters? Quietly, please."

Martin rolled his eyes, but nevertheless plodded over to the cot, Wyatt following close behind. They lugged it to the door, coaxed it clumsily through the opening, and continued out into the sun.

"What's your name?" Wyatt asked as they awkwardly made their way across the village square.

"Martin."

"Oh! Of course," Wyatt smiled. "I'm Wyatt."

"Yeah, I know that," he replied sourly.

Wyatt swallowed. "Oh. I guess my reputation precedes me."

Martin could have said the same thing about Wyatt's recognition, but let that irksome thought slide. "Well, you're kind of a big deal at the moment," Martin muttered. "Barging into this village uninvited and all."

Wyatt frowned, but was silent. They reached a cottage, and dropped the cot on the ground as Wyatt reached for the door. "This is it," he said. "Paul and Mrs. Potter live here. I'm staying with them."

"How interesting," Martin replied stiffly.

Wyatt raised his eyebrows. "You know, maybe if you tried being nice to people, your breath wouldn't be wasted quite so much."

Martin glared at him. "Well, I'm not about to be nice to you, am I?" he spat.

"Why not?"

"I'm not even nice to the locals. Why would I be nice to a foreigner?"

Wyatt looked at him in surprise. He shook his head, fumbling with his end of the bed. "I don't understand this idea of picking sides. Western Village versus Southern Village… all villages versus each other… it's the most ridiculous thing I've ever heard."

Martin held the other end of the bed, putting forth the minimum amount of effort required for the job, as Wyatt tried to angle his end to fit through the doorway. "What's not to understand?" Martin drawled. "For one thing, you foreigners are cracked. Usin' shovels to dig, refusin' us our resources… I even heard the Northern Village prays to the First Man. Like that's gonna do anything." He shook his head. "And speakin' of the Northern Village…

no one ever came to help us when we needed it most. Seems to me like that's a pretty unforgiving quality."

Wyatt furrowed his brow — the bed didn't seem to want to fit — and shook his head. "What could you have possibly needed help with that has gotten you all in a fuss? We're not above helping people, you know. If you all had come to us asking for resources, I'm sure we would give them to you."

Martin rolled his eyes. "You speak like a true child."

Wyatt glared at him, but held his tongue. Martin realized what he had just said and gave a small snort, recognizing the irony. He was essentially a child in a man's body, developmentally. But he still apparently had more of a grip on reality than this kid. Martin hadn't even been out of the mud for a month, and he had already caught up on the village politics — this kid had to be actively avoiding the problem if he didn't have a clue. "There's a lot that you don't understand, kid. Maybe it's because you're not in need. But your folk are like warlords over there, withholdin' and claimin' their privilege. Makes you wish you'd 'a stayed under that field, just to stay out of the war zone."

Wyatt glanced up, surprised. "Well… no. Not exactly. I'd rather be fully conscious, thank you."

Martin dropped his end of the cot, scoffing at Wyatt through the doorway. "You

Western Villagers, you have no respect. What's so wrong about returning to your womb?"

Wyatt scrunched his nose up. "I don't know, Martin, have you liked being under the mud for what, thirty years? Was that enjoyable to you?"

Martin faltered. He remembered back to when he was a boy — almost impossible to remember by now, but he had a vague recollection — when the children were gathered round at celebrations, and stories were told about the field. You didn't need to fear the field, they said, because it was your origin — you were a part of it. But that didn't make Martin's current situation any happier, now, did it? He still had years missing from his life; he was still an underdeveloped middle-aged man. He couldn't exactly say that made him happy.

Martin had tried so very hard to make peace with his situation. He had thrown himself into the jobs he was given, but none seemed to be suited to him; and beyond that, there was that damn disconnect. Get up, go to work, mind the people mumbling greetings to you and then never engaging in conversation after that... Martin felt like he had been thrust into a world that was no longer his. Maybe it never had been.

Wyatt had made his comments off the cuff, but Martin's face instantly told him that it was the biggest mistake he could make. Suddenly Martin wasn't irritable and cross;

he was upset. Wyatt could see him swallowing, over and over again, as if that would preoccupy him from running away. "I'm sorry," Wyatt said quickly, though he knew the words had little value.

"Well, it's better than dealin' with this shit," Martin spat out suddenly, allowing anger to replace his vulnerability. "You people are all so damn full of yourselves. Anybody who's different is nothing to you people. I've been above the mud for a little over a month, and in that short time I have felt nothin' but the slow drain of humanity. Because I don't *belong*, because I stick out like a sore thumb. That's what this place does to you. And I'm talkin' about all the villages, not just this damn one. Judgin' people just because they don't do things the way you like 'em... You know, whatever kind of life I had under the mud, whether it was heaven or hell I'll probably never know; but maybe I would've had more peace of mind if I'd just stayed under. But no, I'm up and walkin' around this damn place... and for what? Tell me! Why are we like this? There's no purpose to this place. We wake up, we eat, we dig, we breathe, we go back to sleep. We fall into fields of mud. There is no meaning to it all!"

He glanced up to see Wyatt staring at him, wide eyed. There was a silence, in which Martin so desperately wished to crawl under the cot jammed inside the doorway — just to remove himself from the intensity of Wyatt's gaze. Instead he turned and walked away, ignoring Wyatt's calls as he blindly walked through the village, a wave of helplessness flowing over him.

He didn't mean to say such nasty things; they came to him naturally, a reflex that he couldn't prevent. It was who he was. Maybe he hadn't been like that before he had fallen under the mud... but he was like that now. But regardless of the impulses that Martin felt, it still hurt to see just how much he didn't belong here. It wasn't that they weren't accepting of him, though he certainly believed that they weren't... it was that he felt like he was supposed to be somewhere else. He felt as if his life was on hold, as if he had been ripped from it. Maybe that was how others who had been under the mud for so long felt.

But he wondered if others felt that same urge to go back to the mud.

♦

A strange tension filled the air on the day of the village's monthly celebration. Many concluded that it was the presence of the foreigners putting a damper on the fun, and many just recognized that it was a severe decrease in newcomers that made the night's festivities seem lacking.

Nonetheless, chairs were set out, and food was lavishly splayed across the tables. The dancing began early enough, lit up by lanterns hung from trees around the village square. The younger folk flocked in gaggles to the dance floor, laughing and hooting, making foolish, lighthearted movements and hopping back and forth between each foot as the band played. The more experienced dancing was a few yards off, with actual steps and routines. A few couples slow-danced, despite the upbeat tempo of the music.

In the past, Mukisa had spent most of the celebrations playing with Cecilia and the other children, gladly reverting back into childhood for the night. Usually Paul would only have to succumb to one dance, which he gladly participated in as long as he could quickly retreat to the side of the dance floor as soon as it was over. Mukisa never asked him for more than that, knowing that one dance was already asking a lot.

But tonight, Paul had already been dragged out onto the dance floor several times. He bore it, knowing the meaning behind Mukisa's excessive energy: he didn't expect to see her playing with the children any time soon. Their games were all too familiar, and all too reminiscent of the presence of her sister. So he made no objection as time and time again he felt her hands pulling him into the arms of the music, spinning him around and then drawing him close, her movements frivolous and playful but her eyes begging him to distract her, to just be close so she would not feel lost.

After a particularly long bout of dancing, Paul found himself alone on the sidelines, finally able to take a breath and simply watch. His relief, however, only lasted so long.

"What I wouldn't give to be that young again."

Paul turned to see Chancellor beside him, staring out at the crowd. He had a smile on his face, but Paul could see it was a front. Casually talking to your daughter's betrothed for the first time? No, no, Chancellor was reaching. He had to be nervous as hell. Paul smiled back at him, soothing his worry for at least a moment. "Mama Nina said that young *and* old must dance. I'm afraid I'm already feeling like the latter... my feet must've fallen off about a half an hour ago."

"You can't be much older than twenty-five... don't mock me," Chancellor grumbled light-heartedly.

Paul sobered, clearing his throat. "Mukisa may not take too kindly to this conversation."

"Yeah, well, Mukisa doesn't take too kindly to much," Chancellor said, shaking his head. "But apparently she took kindly to you."

Paul had no response. Chancellor's gaze remained on the crowd, avoiding his glance at all costs. Paul watched the man become restless — his bravery in initiating the conversation had just soured, and he could sense a retreat coming soon. Better to end on a good note, he thought. "It's a shame we haven't really talked yet, sir," he said, holding out his hand.

Chancellor looked down at the offering, stared it for a moment, and then grasped it firmly in his own hand and shook it. "Are you treating her right?"

"The best."

"I hope it continues that way. Otherwise… I know where you live."

Paul smiled. Chancellor released his hand, nodded, and drifted off into the crowd.

Paul glanced over at Mukisa, who had her arms wrapped around her mother's shoulders, grinning from ear to ear as the two of them conversed with Mama Nina. They looked so alike, her mother and her: the same dark skin, the same shining eyes and sharp features… and they also held the same trait of stubbornness. It may not have been as noticeable with Marie, but they were both firm in their beliefs, and even firmer in their attitudes; it was just *what kind* of attitude that differed between the two of them: the attitude that drew together the strength to mend a broken family, contrasted with the attitude that pushed aside the broken bit that had fallen away and now returned. Reconciling the whole family now would mean rebuilding everything that the last five years had brought to the table for these two women.

He approached them, still lost in thought. Mukisa quickly flitted from her mother's side to his as soon as she saw him pushing through the wandering celebrators. "Another dance?"

Paul gave her an exasperated look. "I think I'm good, thanks."

Mukisa frowned, but didn't say anything. She turned back to her mother. "We're going to get more food, are you hungry?"

Marie shook her head. Mukisa took Paul by the hand, and the two of them wandered over to the table of food, which was beginning to dwindle down. There was, however, still a good portion of a large roast beast on the table, stuffed with apples and spices, and Paul sliced off a piece for the two of them to share. "Are you having fun?" he asked.

"Of course," she said quickly. He glanced at her, searching her face, and she looked away. "Well, truthfully, I'm not having as *much* fun as I usually do."

"Oh?"

Mukisa grimaced. He was doing that thing again, that trying-to-get-her-to-open-up thing. "I just usually don't have as much free time during the celebrations, is all."

Their conversation was cut short by a pair of girls who approached the food table, one pushing the other forward — the latter seemingly quite uncomfortable about it, the former with a smug look on her face. This one began the conversation. "Hello, Mukisa," she remarked wryly. "Did you slay this beast for us tonight?"

Mukisa gave her a withering look. "Think

about what you're asking, Caroline," she said. "We kill more game in a week than you could count in your head, and you're expecting me to recognize if this happens to be one of the things I caught?"

"Oh, but Mukisa, you should be proud of the work you do," Caroline replied with mock encouragement. "Don't you think, Rosie?" Her friend quickly lowered her eyes to the ground.

Mukisa and Paul exchanged glances. Caroline was the queen of belittlement, without ever actually saying negative words. It was the tone of her voice that made you feel like an outcast... which wasn't, Mukisa speculated, that hard in her case.

"Do you have something particular to say, Caroline," Paul piped up, "or are you just trying to be an ass?"

Caroline blinked at Paul's remark, surprised. Beside her, Rosie tugged nervously at her sleeve. "Come on, Caroline, let's leave her alone. Let's go dance."

Caroline elbowed her friend, smirking. "I'm just trying to compliment your betrothed, Paul. She's always done a fantastic job of killing things, don't you think?"

Such a comment was meant to get a rise out of Mukisa, and she did not disappoint: she stepped forward, lowering her glaring face right into Caroline's. Rosie squeaked and jumped away from the two of them, eyes wide.

Mukisa felt Paul's arms around her stomach, dragging her away from the girls, and heard his soothing whisper in her ear: "Not worth it, Mukisa." Seething, she shoved him off of her, but did not return to the table. He was right, of course. Caroline was not worth it. Interestingly enough, however, Rosie's behavior was what was momentarily irking her. "Paul... Did you see that? People are still terrified of me."

Paul raised an eyebrow. "I'm pretty sure Caroline is not terrified of you."

"But Rosie was! Did you see how she was acting? You heard her... she said, 'let's leave *her* alone'. Not '*them*', '*her*'."

Paul sighed. "So what? Does Rosie's opinion really matter that much to you?"

Mukisa rolled her eyes. "No. But if she's still scared of me, then she can't be the only one."

Paul chuckled. "Mukisa, I think a lot of the girls were scared of you long before what happened five years ago."

"I'm sure you mean to be encouraging." She turned and saw Martin standing a few feet away, smirking. "Do you have a comment?" she snapped.

Martin sneered. "Oh, so sad, someone feels different, and doesn't fit in with the other kids."

"Go away, Martin." She grabbed Paul's arm and began dragging him away, but stopped dead at Martin's next words.

"You and I are a lot alike, you know."

She laughed darkly. "I am *nothing* like you."

Martin raised an eyebrow. "And you're really proving your point with that attitude."

Mukisa's eyes flashed, and Paul quickly leaned forward to interfere. "Come on, Mukisa," he said quietly, firmly nudging her away.

They moved to the other side of the square, weaving their way through the crowd. Mukisa glanced back at Martin; he was watching them, with quite a gloomy expression on his face, but when he caught her glance, he quickly focused on the people dancing in the center of the square. She studied him for a moment. No one spoke to him, and the occasional passerby bumped into him, as if he wasn't there. Her spirits had already been low, but somehow they dropped even further as she watched the intolerable man shuffle away through the crowd.

But she was immediately whisked away from her thoughts as Paul grabbed her hand. "Come on," he said. "One more dance. That'll cheer you up."

Mukisa sincerely hoped that would be the case.

◆

And here he found himself again.

Staring at that field like he was meant to be on it, enticed by its alluring voice... Behind him, the celebration continued, as it would until late into the night, no doubt. He could hear the sounds of laughter and music echoing through the trees. No one had even noticed him parting from the crowd; they were too busy cavorting with one another.

Martin grimaced, reaching up and rubbing one shoulder, then the other. They had been giving him pain these last few days. He couldn't recall ever having such knots in his shoulders.

He took a small step forward. The field was last on the list of jobs, but there was no reason he shouldn't step out onto it now. Why not? It wouldn't *harm* him, certainly. Sure, it was nighttime, and the village always said that it was easier to fall under after dark, but would that really be worse than his life above the mud? After all, this was the womb from which they had all been wrought… he didn't believe that it could offer anything less than comfort.

People treated the field like it was to be feared. To be quite honest, Martin didn't really care if it was dangerous or not. After all, he had spent the majority of his life under there, so if there was danger, he clearly had eluded it. And it most certainly was more a home to him than this place. He had spent, what, five years in the Southern Village before falling back under again all those years ago? Those five years were such a blur — he could barely remember what transpired thirty years ago, especially when the memories were clouded by his time in the mud.

He thought he might enjoy that. He tried to imagine what it would be like to forget the past few months over the mud. He had tried so hard to fall into place with the rest of the village: doing their jobs, eating their food, adopting that reverence for the field when all he felt about it was a sort of magnetism. He had thrown himself into their ways, but they still ignored him, and he still was cruel. If the bodies under the mud were unconscious, then at least they weren't feeling pain, feeling loneliness. It would be a relief to not feel anything at all. Certainly better than feeling as useless as he did now.

But it wasn't just the numbing of the senses that Martin longed for; he still felt strangely drawn back to the field, as if he had some kind of unfinished business to attend to under the mud. He could not escape the feeling that maybe he had been prematurely birthed into this disaster that people called home, incomplete and in need of the amniotic fluids that would bring him fully to life. This womb had to finish what it had started in him, whatever that may be.

The villagers would have a thing or two to say about him stepping out onto the field. But it wasn't as if it would definitely mean that he would fall under... that was just a possibility, just one of many things that may happen. And if it happened, so what? Good riddance. He could risk losing these insufferable people for company, if it meant giving himself a little adventure.

Yes, stepping out onto the field would be an adventure. For that is what risks are, he thought.

His toes were at the very edge of the field. He gave a small smile. He tried to think of the last time he had smiled. He couldn't recall it. Maybe he had never smiled — maybe he had lived his whole life without smiling. How fitting it was that he smiled now. Maybe it was a sign that this is what he needed to do.

He took a step out onto the field, and cringed, waiting.

Nothing.

His smile spread further across his face.

He took another step out, reveling in the sucking pull of the mud, the uneven ground that he had come to tread on. Another step. Another moment, and suddenly he was in the middle of the field.

♦

Mukisa found herself gravitating towards the field. She wasn't sure why she wanted to go there… perhaps it was to will Cecilia up from its midst. Get away from the loneliness of the party, and plead with the field to release her sister.

But when she arrived at the edge of the field, Cecilia left her mind. Standing on the field, a few yards from the safety of the edge, was Martin. Even with his back turned she could tell it was him — that slouched, sulking demeanor was a dead giveaway.

She sighed. She didn't want to deal with Martin's nonsense right now. But before she could silently sneak away, Martin turned, and Mukisa realized he had been crying — his eyes were red.

Martin frowned at her. "What?" he spat. "What do you want?"

Mukisa squinted at him. No, his eyes weren't just red from crying — the pupils were red, too. The sight brought her to a halt a few yards away. There was something familiar about those red eyes; but more than familiarity, they brought a chill to her body. "Are... you okay?" she asked with trepidation.

Martin glowered at her. He turned and continued walking toward the center of the field.

♦

Martin's mind was buzzing. No, echoing — like his conscience was yelling. He could hear it as if it was actually happening, a nagging thing, telling him to get off the field.

Get off the field.

It's off limits after dark, you useless fool.

Who do you think you are?

Stop causing so much trouble.

You waste of space.

What the hell for?! he thought, balling up

his fists. I'm not doing anything else that needs to be done, so why can't I do this one thing?

He glanced back at Mukisa behind him. She had that damn bead strewn across her forehead. Well, wasn't it nice that she had her life all figured out? That she belonged? Martin felt a tear trickling down the side of his face. Wasn't it just fantastic that she got a family, a real one, one that she complained about, no less, and he was stuck with no one, all by himself in a field full of mud with no memory of who he was and no hope for who he would become…

The excitement of the field wore off in an instant, and in its place came a sudden drain of energy, a sinking, heavy weight on his chest, expanding, a rush of nausea. He wanted to just get it over with. Maybe falling under *would* be better than this life. If you could call it life.

He glanced up at the sky. Several specters had risen from their roosts, watching him with their beady little glowing eyes. They flew in circles, swooping lower and lower, slowly descending towards the field.

He heard a yell, the words of which his brain wasn't cooperative enough to process, and saw more villagers coming, dotting the edge of the field with angry looks on their faces.

Suddenly the ground beneath him began to shift, at first ever so slightly, and then in greater and greater rocking motions. Martin felt like he was on a boat. He threw his arms out to steady himself, and looked up at the people surrounding the field. Their looks of anger had quickly changed to looks of surprise, of worry. Ha! Now he had their attention.

But now the specters were circling only a few feet above his head. And the mud was beginning to ripple, the field to pulsate. He had awakened it. Or had he? Maybe he had only awakened a section of the mud — it looked like it was only moving around him. The rest of the field remained dead still. A few people had begun to run towards him, unaffected by any rolls or waves of mud.

It was at this point that Martin began to feel nervous.

And the next thing he knew, cold wings were slapping against his skin, the force knocking him backward — he was falling, the field had scooped him up and tossed him into itself, mud striking the side of his face, seeping into his open, screaming mouth, into his ears, flooding through the cracks in his grasping fingers, his arm movements hindered by its thickness, and he couldn't break his fall, couldn't prevent himself from sinking further and further, and he felt hands grasping at his receding body, the villagers must have reached him, *oh please get me out*, and then—

♦

The villagers raced onto the field, yelling and waving their fists at the specters, which quickly picked themselves up and flew off into the night, screeching. They left almost too quickly.

Mukisa reached the spot in the mud where Martin's body had made a small dent at about the same time as several other villagers. They began to dig deep into the mud, one hand after the other, but Martin's body had so quickly receded that she knew it was a lost cause. She was sure the others around her could see it too, but continued digging nonetheless.

Suddenly Mukisa stopped digging, feeling a rumbling. The mud began to bubble around her, and she jumped to her feet, eyes wide. The other villagers around her began to scream, and everyone backed away from the piece of field into which Martin had disappeared. And suddenly, all of them grew silent, for there was another sound that they were preoccupied with.

It was the sound of a deep, guttural scream, unearthly, nothing they had ever heard before, and it was coming from under the mud.

It was drawn out, getting louder and louder, until suddenly...

Silence.

Mukisa quickly followed the rest of the village in running off of the field as fast as they could. She spun around, and stared back out at the spot they had come from: there was one more little ripple, and then the field was still.

6

The Need

"The field is off limits after dark. Everyone knew that, and Martin knew that."

"Still, I feel that we should reiterate the dangers."

"No need. Everyone saw what happened."

Mukisa sat in the grass, leaning against the Guest House, and listening in on the conversation inside. The village elders were having a meeting about Martin.

She couldn't focus on their words. The only thing that held her attention at that moment was the field. Poor Martin. She had never liked him, of course — he was as ill-tempered and nasty as she was half the time —

but maybe that was why she felt sorry for him now. She could understand his misery. She had known he wasn't fitting in; and rightly so, for if she hadn't been able to experience the better part of her growing years, she would probably not even know how to act around even her own mother.

No one had *wanted* Martin to fall under years ago, but it had happened, and the village had adapted. So when Martin finally resurfaced, it was an inadvertent isolation: he didn't fit in and didn't feel like a part of the village, but no one was casting him out... he was just there. People acknowledged his existence, but they didn't really know what to do with him.

Mukisa had had her own fair share of social anxiety. As anyone in the village could attest, she wasn't the easiest to converse with — her hot temper usually got in the way of any bonding that a relationship needed to continue past the occasional "hello". It was a mystery how Paul had succeeded... perhaps it was that she could never get him to speak more than five words at a time — no one could, really, and that was the key — and so it almost became a mission to have a conversation with him every time they crossed paths. He had somehow broken through to her heart in his quiet, endearing way.

But Martin had had no one. His adopted parents had both died several years ago of old age — he didn't even have a mother to go crying to when the children wouldn't play with him. Of course, by the time he was back up out of the mud, he was long past nursery rhymes and games of tag, but… she could feel his loneliness now, as if it had escaped his body the moment he returned to the mud, and was trying to find a new home inside of her.

She knew that hurt he had felt. The one that had driven him to his fall into the mud. But the difference between her and Martin was that Mukisa would continue to push against that pain, to drive it out. Maybe Martin had never really learned to do that.

People were saying that Martin hadn't been ready to come back up from the mud, to return to society. The field hadn't finished with him. Mukisa didn't understand how long was enough.

His eyes kept resurfacing in her mind, from right before he fell under. Why had the pupils been red?

She shivered, and felt a strong pair of arms wrap a blanket around her shoulders. "What did I miss?" Paul asked, sitting beside her.

Mukisa rolled her eyes. "A whole lot of nothing. Just a bunch of people trying to push the blame onto others." Paul nodded, raising an eyebrow, and Mukisa pressed her toes into the grass thoughtfully. "I wish my sister was here."

Paul was silent for a moment. She looked at him, and saw that his eyes were glossy with empathy. She sighed. "Maybe the field will do a trade and give Cecilia back. It gets one body back, and returns another, yeah?"

Paul continued to just stare at her. She pursed her lips. "I hate it when you do this."

"Do what?"

"Not say anything. And then I talk and talk until I come up with an answer in my head that makes everything feel a little better, except that I don't want to be consoled, Paul. I want my sister to come back."

He lowered his gaze to the ground, furrowing his brow. He was trying to find a way to fix things, and was drawing a blank. Paul was not very good at fixing things. But he was, Mukisa had to admit, a hell of a listener.

♦

Mukisa sat, silently cooking breakfast. She had found herself dangerously low on water for boiling this morning, so instead of the usual morning porridge, today it would be eggs and bacon — a special treat. The irony of the situation felt especially ripe. Mindlessly pushing the food around on the clay cooking slab, she watched as the rest of the villagers awakened and came out of their houses, beginning their morning routines. The air was so pleasant, the sun beating down on them so cheerfully as if last week's fall had never happened.

But despite the amiable weather, Mukisa

felt tired; the night had been long, and full of too many unwanted thoughts. Since the diggers from the Western Village had invaded their space, Mukisa had been on edge. She wasn't even necessarily afraid that they would bring trouble to the village... they had, after all, made their intentions clear. Perhaps she was just being paranoid about the presence of strangers. And she wasn't used to sharing space; every time she went to Paul's house, there was Wyatt, the most frustratingly enthusiastic kid she had ever met. She even noticed that it was putting Paul on edge too; although perhaps it wasn't his enthusiasm, but just the fact that an extra body was in his home every night.

Mukisa watched the boy now, playing catch with a group of children on the green. Wyatt threw a piece of fruit into the air, causing the children to nearly trip over themselves in pursuit, giggling and pushing each other out of the way.

She watched the scene in puzzlement. Here he was, only a couple of years younger than her, and he had somehow managed to keep himself free from the controversial politics between the villages, making friends with strangers almost instantly. Granted, it was the children he had befriended, who were also unaware of the differences between themselves and their new friend, but... Mukisa couldn't imagine going to another village and fitting right in. She barely fit into her own home.

Catherine, the little girl from the Guest House, was amongst the group of children. It seemed that she hadn't yet found her place amongst the children; in this particular game, she was far too little to catch the fruit, her reaching hands still about a foot shorter than those of the older children in the group, and no one seemed willing to go out of their way to include her. Mukisa watched as she slowly became downhearted and separated from the others, kicking at the grass scornfully.

Wyatt noticed too. "Hey! Catch!"

Catherine turned as Wyatt threw the fruit in her direction. She caught it, smiling shyly.

Wyatt was clearly proud of himself; he grinned and tousled the hair of a little boy standing next to him. Suddenly the fruit smacked him in the face, and he blinked. And there was Catherine, doubled over with laughter, the other children joining in at her bravery.

Mukisa could not share in their smiles. All she could do was picture Cecilia amongst them.

She rolled her eyes, jabbing the embers of her fire with a stick. She needed to hurry up and get ready for work, or else she would find herself preoccupied with thoughts of her sister for the rest of the day.

Glancing up, she saw her mother a few yards off, staring up at the sky with an expression that Mukisa had learned long ago was either boredom or worry. And Mama was rarely bored.

She scraped the eggs and bacon off of the cooking slab and put half on a plate, making her way over to her mother. "Eat," she said, smiling, and her mother took the plate with a nod before turning again to silently regard the sky. Mukisa frowned. "What's the matter?"

"There are no rain clouds." She gave a sigh. "We're going to have to fetch water."

♦

The whole village trudged through the forest, some pulling carts of large jugs and buckets behind them, others carrying the smaller jugs in their arms. The sun weaseled its way through the protection of the trees as they walked, making them blink. It was just enough of an annoyance to cause the villagers to look forward to the walk home: though they would be carrying a heavier load, they would at least find relief in having their backs to the sun.

Wyatt awkwardly adjusted the jug he held, trying not to drop it as they walked. A crow squawked nearby, and he flinched at the sudden noise, quickly glancing around to discover its source. He gave a frustrated sigh. "Can anyone explain to me why the entire village is taking a little trek through a forest full of wild and dangerous animals?" he asked.

Mukisa and Paul walked behind Wyatt; Mukisa let out a snort. "Take a look at what's in your hands. We're going to collect water. We don't have a nice little pipe system like you do."

Wyatt stopped, surprised, and the two of them nearly ran straight into him. "Why the hell not?"

Mukisa glared at him, her irritation apparent. "Because you won't share your resources!"

Wyatt stared at her. "What do you mean?"

Paul offered a wary smile, glancing hastily between the two of them. "Mayor Kenton brings the supplies for the pipe systems — the metal and all that — on his trips. But we haven't had the pleasure of his presence in the village for a little over a year, and he didn't bring much more than a basket full of supplies. And even if he did bring more... your village has claimed the nearest pond as your own."

"Which you have so gracefully allowed us to borrow water from," Mukisa added spitefully.

Wyatt was still confused. "It's a natural resource, isn't it? How could we lay claim over a pond?"

Mukisa sized him up, as if contemplating whether he was worth punching in the face. "With things like this," she said, nodding to the knife tucked under her belt. Wyatt swallowed uncomfortably.

She pushed past him roughly, and Paul followed after her, giving Wyatt an apologetic look as he passed.

Up ahead, Chancellor and Marie walked beside each other. Chancellor couldn't help but smile, walking through this path that he had so often trod in the past.

"Remember when we would make this trip early just to be alone?" Chancellor asked, smiling at her. "No matter that we could have gotten ourselves killed, out in the middle of this godforsaken forest."

Marie gave him a tired glance, her response delayed. "Yes, I do."

"I wouldn't have let anything hurt you out here, of course," Chancellor said quickly.

Marie had no response for that, and just stared ahead as they walked, leaving Chancellor to scramble for something to fill the silence.

"I think we're getting close to the part of the trail that we would try to race—"

"Yes, Chancellor, we are." Marie quickly pushed past him and joined the group of villagers up ahead, her face an indecipherable rock. Chancellor sighed.

A few moments later, the group of travelers came to a halt as several Western Villagers appeared amongst the trees. "Gate check," Mama Nina called out, putting her hand on a young one's shoulder to slow him in

107

his playful running.

Marie and Chancellor stepped into line with each other to greet the guards. "We're here to fill up and leave," Marie said simply.

One of the guards saw Chancellor. "Sheriff? Are you accompanying them?" he asked in disbelief.

Chancellor nodded. "I have not found my daughter yet. Until then, their need of water is my need of water."

The guard thought for a moment, glancing at John and Wyatt, who were further in amongst the crowd of Southern Villagers. "You seem to be blending in well," he muttered, but moved aside for the caravan to pass through.

The line of villagers pushed through to a clearing, where a large pond awaited them. Some began to fill their buckets; others took time to enjoy the cool feel of the water around their feet. The children dropped their jugs on the ground and picked up their games from earlier in the day, much to the dismay of their parents, who warned them to stay near the clearing. All the while, the guards from the Western Village watched them with a careful eye from various points around the clearing's edge.

On the opposite side of the pond, several pipes weaved their way through the hills and into the forest beyond, guarded at various points by villagers on duty. Those pipes would travel about two miles before they hit the Western Village; Marie studied them from afar, idly wondering if the four miles that it had taken them to arrive here from the Southern Village was too great a distance for a similar setup. With the right tools, perhaps it wasn't. And she was getting tired of watching the sky... it was always a frustrating day when she would see rain clouds in the distance, drifting right in the direction of the Western Village, but narrowly missing the village that desperately needed them. The Southern Village was for some reason cursed with reliving that scenario over and over. It had happened just a few days prior... the night that Cecilia had fallen. A particularly malicious omen.

Marie shuddered and tore her eyes from the pipes. Her gaze landed on Chancellor, who had stopped a few feet away from her, also staring out across the pond. For a fleeting moment, he even looked a little guilty.

"Did you ever petition your people?" Marie asked.

"Of course I did," Chancellor replied quickly.

"You made a promise, Chancellor. A promise that you would convince them to share the pipes. Five years later, and where are we?"

"These things take time — you don't actually think they would have been willing, after what happened?"

Marie raised her eyebrows. "I would

watch what you say, Sheriff."

He sighed. "It's not that I blame you — there was already tension between the villages before—"

"So the reality is," Marie interjected impatiently, "that you never pressed the matter. They said they didn't want to share the pipes, and you said, fine, whatever you wish."

Chancellor glared at her. "I do what I need to do in order to help my people. They come first."

Marie stared at him for a moment, taken aback. She blinked, and composed herself. "And neighbors are supposed to come second. Or at least they were at some point, right? And yet the Western Village is well off, and we still desperately need our water."

Chancellor continued to stare ahead for a moment. He seemed determined not to give her the satisfaction of getting to him. Marie shook her head, smoothing the folds of her dress. "Ah, but maybe your people are not to blame. Right? So if sharing is too difficult for you... Maybe next time you see Mayor Kenton, you could mention to him that the Southern Village is living without. At least warn him that such matters are grinding the nerves of one quarter of the village, one quarter who will be looking to replace him when the time comes. I'm sure that will spur him into action."

Chancellor shook his head. "I don't know the next time I'll see him."

"And yet it'll still be before we do. I'm not

asking you to save us, I'm just asking you to give us a chance."

Chancellor stared at the ground, and Marie walked away, grabbing a jug as she went. She stopped and turned back, giving him a withering look. "*Your people*, Chancellor? I don't recall you being such an ass five years ago."

Chancellor stood there for a moment, at a loss for what to do. Finally he turned and looked out at the crowd of villagers, all enjoying their trip to the waterfront. At another spot by the pond, he saw Mukisa and Paul standing ankle deep in the water, talking.

Chancellor approached them warily. "Mukisa?" Mukisa stiffened at the sound of his voice, refusing to turn around. "Can we talk?"

There was a hesitation, and then she allowed herself to turn a little as she responded, though not fully toward him — she wouldn't give him even that. "I'm sorry, I'm talking to my betrothed right now."

She turned back away from him and began to whisper to Paul again. However, Paul would have no part in this game; he glared at her and abruptly walked away, leaving her to stare after him in a panic. Chancellor smiled inwardly. Well, at least someone was on his side.

Mukisa quickly composed herself enough to glare at her father, though her momentary turmoil still flickered across her face. Chancellor knew that look; he had seen it countless times when, as a young girl, Mukisa was caught doing something she wasn't supposed to do. It was that cross between defiance, believing she had every right to the thing she was doing, and uncertainty — had she miscalculated? Maybe she should've thought of the repercussions of this action before she went ahead and did it. Chancellor watched his daughter storm away in a huff, and couldn't help but smile. He missed these interactions with his daughter, exasperating or not.

♦

Paul sat on a fallen tree at another spot by the pond, thinking. He had made it a point to quickly and effectively remove himself from the conversation between his betrothed and her father — he wanted nothing to do with it. He had a feeling it hadn't lasted long, judging by the look on Mukisa's face when Chancellor had approached them.

Peering through the trees, Paul saw Wyatt and John, talking and laughing with one of the guards. They seemed to have fallen right in amongst their people; though to be fair, they had been gone for a week. There was surely a lot to catch up on.

Paul lowered his head into his hands; the past few days had made it really start to spin, and he wanted a break from it. Not only was the introduction of the foreigners stressful, but the relationship between Mukisa and her father was enough to make a man crazy. He wished things could have happened one problem at a time.

The thing was, he wasn't sure what he was supposed to make of Chancellor. He was Mukisa's father — he should be grateful that he brought her into the world, no matter what the village said about the oddity of flesh-born children. But he had deserted her... and that was something that did not resonate well with Paul. But maybe he just didn't know the whole story; maybe there was some redeeming factor in Chancellor that he had yet to discover. After all, the Western Village had chosen him as their sheriff, so he must have some reputable quality about him... unless they had just chosen him haphazardly. And who knew? It was possible. Paul was not one to quickly judge the other villages, but it didn't mean that there were instances in which he could not help it.

But did it even matter whether or not he was a good person? Paul was, after all, pushing his way into the man's family, regardless of how disconnected the man may be to them. He sighed. He almost wished that Mukisa and her father could simply find common ground, just so that Paul wouldn't have to decide what to feel.

"Now you see what you're getting yourself into."

Paul looked up and saw Mama Nina

smiling at him from just a few yards away. He shook his head sadly. She slowly made her way over to him, adjusted her long robes, and sat beside him on the tree. "Tell me your worries."

He laughed. Here she was, trying to play the part of a mother again. Mama Nina had been like a mother to him since the day he had been unearthed. More than once he had caught himself, very ashamedly, wondering why she couldn't have adopted him instead of his own Mama. He loved his adoptive mother, but she was not one for deep conversations. Instead, she was full of encouragement, for which Paul was grateful; but Mama Nina was extraordinarily gifted at forcing Paul to think… and she certainly knew the right moments to use this gift. "Ah, so you want me to complain," he teased.

"It's only complaining if you aren't humble about it," she mused. "There's a fine line between complaining and confiding. You choose what you are about to do."

He shook his head. "Where should I start?"

"You can start wherever you like. The middle, the end…" She smiled. "You can even start at the beginning."

"Well…" He wasn't even sure what the beginning of his thoughts should be. He shrugged. "Shouldn't I be worrying about whether I'm making a good impression on the father? Instead of whether the father is making a good impression on the daughter?"

"Every family has its baggage."

"Yeah, but with Mukisa, it's more intensified."

Mama nodded, chuckling. "So you are unsure about what to think of Chancellor Wallheart. I think the fact that he's even here at least means that he cares."

"That's true." He put his head in his hands, frustrated. "And yet she won't see that."

A glint came to Mama's eye. "And that is what makes her who she is."

"And that is who I want to marry." He sighed. "What do I do, Mama?"

She thought for a moment. "This is not for me to decide. I don't know that it's even for you to decide. This is a matter that lies in her hands. If she wants to make amends with her father, she will." She smiled, and patted his hand. "But you can't force her to make amends, or even to hurry up the process. She must make up her own mind. You take pride, Paul, in being the flagpole to the flag; but the wind will still take it where it wants to go. All you can do is hold on."

Paul nodded, staring out at the water bleakly. "I'm sure that's meant to make me feel better."

"It's meant to let you know it's not your battle. I can do nothing about how you feel."

They sat for a moment, enjoying the silence that they shared, listening to the birds sing their songs and watching as the other villagers whiled the time away in the cool waters of the pond. Then, as everyone finished their idling and began collecting their jugs, they joined the crowd and began their walk back through the forest.

♦

The day resumed as normal as soon as they returned to the village. Everyone went about their daily jobs, throwing themselves into the work now that they had lost some time from their day trip.

Marie leisurely patrolled the field, watching the diggers as they toiled under the hot sun. Chancellor was in their midst, working just as hard as the rest of them. If she let her imagination wander, she could pretend that it was almost twenty years ago, when she had first met him. He had been a visitor too, just like she had been, though his traveling had been for fun and hers... well, hers had not. But Marie had already made the Southern Village her home by the time he had arrived; she had been living there for about a year and, given the circumstances, there was no other place she would rather be. She remembered seeing him on the field, helping the diggers in exchange for a place to stay for the night, and thinking, he's going to be just like me — he's going to stick around. She wasn't sure how she knew, but she had a gut feeling... or maybe it was more like a promise than intuition, for when he had finished his work on the field later that day, she had made sure to bump into him and introduce herself.

Chancellor glanced up at her as he dug, and she quickly looked away. No need to get it into his head that she was watching him. He already seemed to want to fit himself right back into her family's life, and she was not too keen on that idea.

Instead, she directed her attention to John and Wyatt, who approached the field with blunted shovels in hand. She held her breath, putting two and two together: they must have brought the shovels from the Western Village, because they certainly didn't use shovels here.

The rest of the diggers stopped and stared at them warily. Marie could see it in their eyes: they had allowed these foreigners to stay in their village, eat their food, and drink their precious water, but this was crossing the line. She cleared her throat and stepped forward. "You can't use those here, boys," she said quietly, hoping against hope that she could settle the issue without raising the entire village to alert.

"What do you mean?" John asked, narrowing his eyes.

"She means," said Chancellor, standing from his spot on the field, "that shovels are prohibited on this field."

Marie calmly took Wyatt's shovel from him and dropped it on the ground. She reached for John's shovel, but he pulled it from her reach defensively. "It's faster."

Marie smiled at him. "Yes, it's faster. But it is also leaves the people we're trying to unearth with mutilated bodies."

"If you're not careful, yes—"

"Nothing unnatural is allowed on this field, you can't just bring your foreign practices to *our* village—"

"If you actually trained your diggers, you'd come to realize it's much more efficient—"

Chancellor let out a loud whistle, drawing everyone's attention. So much for keeping things quiet. They stared silently at him, Wyatt with wide eyes.

Chancellor stepped forward, giving John a look. "John. We're in the Southern Village. We will do as the Southern Village does."

"That's bird shit!"

"*John*." His voice was quiet but firm. John glared at him, and threw his shovel to the ground furiously. He and Wyatt crossed onto the field and joined the digging. Marie nodded to Chancellor, loosening her grip on the baton in the folds of her dress. She was not sure if she should be grateful or irritated that his authority had been more effective than hers. But then, they were his villagers... of course they would heed his words first. She sighed and left them to their work.

Today, the diggers battled not only with the mud but also with the sun. It was especially hot today — they all murmured in agreement that today would have been much worse without a trip to the pond — and it seemed to be making the specters overhead a little antsy. Four of them hung low in the sky, circling and whispering to each other in the strange, murmuring tone that they conversed with. For all the sun that beat down on the villagers, it certainly didn't seem sunny with the specters so close.

"Look at 'em, spying on us," Wyatt muttered, wiping his brow. "Southern Village has got some anxious specters."

John looked up at the beasts, then turned to Wyatt, leaning in close. "They're not watching us," he whispered, "they're watching the locals." He laughed. "I think we can trust the specters more than we can the Southies." Wyatt gave him a puzzled look, but John didn't seem to notice it; he wiped his brow and stared up at the sky. "You know, they say there used to be loads more specters."

"When?"

"I don't know. Way far back. Back in the time of the First Man."

Wyatt thought for a moment. "Maybe they're becoming extinct."

John chuckled. "Wouldn't that be nice?" he said, and the two of them continued digging.

Wyatt was still thinking about the specters when he suddenly uncovered a mess of fingers, squirming desperately in the mud. He reached down and took hold of the muddied hand, and it patted his fingers eagerly, feeling, identifying. Grasping it, he pulled, planting his feet around the hand and sinking them into the mud for a little bit of stability. The hand led to an arm, and that led to a shoulder. Then the face emerged, a girl's face, eyes wide as if absorbing the sunlight, mud oozing off her cheeks. A gasp came from the girl's mouth, and her eyelids fluttered, her hand tightened around Wyatt's.

The second hand emerged, taking hold of Wyatt's other, then one elbow, which began digging at the mud around it. It was a struggle against the sucking mud, and the girl was losing.

"Can I get some help over here?!" Wyatt yelled out, struggling.

John looked over and stood to help, when suddenly, with a wrenching abruptness, the newcomer was yanked downward, her hands slipping from Wyatt's grasp.

Wyatt shouted and lunged forward, pawing at the hole, which was swallowing itself rapidly. Feeling a small, receding solid surface, perhaps a finger, he thought, he sprawled out on his stomach and reached his arm all the way in after it.

"No!" John rushed over just as Wyatt tipped and fell into the mud face first.

Mud gurgled past his ears, plugging his nose and seeping through the cracks of his mouth. He felt strong hands from behind grab his legs, pulling, and his downward fall slowed.

Abruptly, the mud gave way to clear blue water. It was an eerie blue, stretching out in every direction. Wyatt gasped involuntarily, inhaling the water and sputtering. He was going to drown! He needed to get back up, go back through the mud and reach air. His head jerked in tune to the flailing of his arms, desperately trying to pull at the wall of mud around his chest, which continued far past the ability of his eyes.

Seconds passed. Wyatt suddenly realized that he was still sucking the water into his lungs, but it didn't hurt. The water was breathable? No. Only partly — he was still short of breath. Nonetheless, he took a deep breath, letting the liquid pour into his mouth and nose. He breathed out — bubbles floated out of his nostrils, and he let out a short laugh.

How could this be? He stopped flailing and peered about him, noticing for the first time the details of his surroundings: bodies floated by, comatose, skin pale and saturated, their limbs slowly drifting at their sides, unperturbed by the stillness of the water. One body drifted into the wall of mud, oblivious. Wyatt's eyes widened at the sight; but of course, it all made sense. This was the Womb; not his, of course, but the Southern Village's Womb. Of course he could breathe this strange liquid. He had been born in it.

He could feel a tingling in his legs, and a thought fluttered dimly into the back of his mind that his fellow diggers were still pulling, trying to rescue him from the mud. Did he have a story to tell them!

But first he wanted to take in his

surroundings. It was strange, but this place felt... relaxing. He felt almost at home, content to sit peacefully and absorb this familiar environment. He almost felt inclined to close his eyes and take a nap. The sensation was a confusing one, contrasting with the bodies around him.

A hand reached out from the wall of mud, catching onto Wyatt's own hand. Wyatt jumped at its touch, then grasped the hand tightly as it began to pull him back through.

A muted shriek came from below, and Wyatt whipped his head around to see a blurry, glowing mass coming at him from the depths of the water. He squinted curiously as he began to inch backward through the wall of mud, trying to make sense of it. It swam closer and closer, until suddenly, it came into focus—

A guttural scream surrounded him, and he wondered if it was coming from his own throat.

♦

John held firmly onto Wyatt's hand, pulling with all his might as the diggers around him excavated the boy from the mud. He was only about a third of the way out, and his head was still mostly submerged — the field was sucking him in hard.

John glanced up to see Chancellor pushing through the crowd that had gathered. He looked — what was it, crestfallen? Probably hoping to see his daughter coming out of the mud — then seemed to brush that thought aside and began to help lift the mud away from the boy.

Wyatt's head popped out of the mud with a smacking sound, and he gasped, wide-eyed, spitting out mud and flopping around what body parts he had available to flop. He looked desperately up at John, who nodded encouragingly and grabbed hold of his arm, heaving upward.

Wyatt's eyes suddenly flicked from John's face to something behind him. A look of even greater terror settled on his face, and he let out a scream. John tore his eyes away from his work and gasped — a specter was rushing toward the field from above, its mouth open wide in a fierce battle cry, its grotesque, narrowed eyes alive with animosity. Diggers dove out of the way as the specter reached the field at an incredible speed, its taloned fingers extended towards the half-uprooted boy. The surrounding diggers began to shout, trying to wave the specter away; but this only angered it more, and attracted its three friends from the sky, who dove after it, swiping at the diggers and making blood fly.

Chancellor scrambled out of the ambush on his elbows, eyes wide. The tangle of arms, legs, and wings throbbed before him, and the rest of the diggers swarmed around the fight, one or two tentatively joining to defend their friends. He couldn't even see the heart of the action anymore, so many were there in the mix.

He jumped up and scanned the edge of the field for Marie, wishing she hadn't taken away his baton. It would have at least given him *something* to ward off the specters with. His eyes locked onto her at the opposite end of the field; she stared at the scene in shock, and hurried onto the field, reaching for her own baton as she approached.

Suddenly there was a terrible shriek from one of the specters — a sound of pain, not a battle cry — and it shot off, away from the group. Chancellor turned back to see what had happened. The crowd of diggers suddenly became very hushed and backed away as, from the thick of things, John came into view. He swung his shovel at the specters, beating them away from the field one by one with delighted vigor. The beasts took off, letting out screams that shook the ground, and disappeared into the sky.

Wyatt lay, still partially entrenched in the mud, deep lacerations covering his face and arms. Blood mingled with mud. He stared helplessly up, watching the specters turn into specks beyond the tops of the trees in the forest. The bloodied diggers turned to stare at John, who spit fiercely into the mud. "No shovels, my ass." He slung the tool over his shoulder, walking away and muttering to himself.

The diggers came back to their senses and

quickly dug Wyatt the rest of the way to safety. After a minute, they had wrenched him from the pull of the field, and he quickly collapsed, tears streaming down his face, ignoring the diggers' requests to maybe not lie back down in the mud, please. He probably didn't even notice their requests... the poor boy was in shock.

7

The Beast

Adranna gathered her things quickly and quietly into a small knapsack. She picked up her mother's old cotton blue dress from the bed and stared down at it, grief momentarily creeping into the corners of her vision. She pressed the cloth to her nose and inhaled — it still had her scent. Her mother may be dead and buried, but she still had one last remnant of her, for a few more days, anyway. And by any means, the dress now fit Adranna; she had now reached the point where she didn't think she'd grow too much more, finally warming up to adulthood. It wasn't the newest of garments, but if she was careful, she could make it last for quite a while.

A noise at the door made her abruptly drop the dress and push her knapsack to the ground. She

*looked up to see Papa standing there, staring at her
with bloodshot eyes. He had a bottle in his hand.
"What are you doin'?"*

"I'm just thinking."

*"What are you thinkin' about?" He dropped the
bottle resolutely, and it smashed on the floor,
making Adranna flinch. He stepped over the splintered
pieces, a serious look on his face. "Were you thinkin'
of leavin'?"*

*Adranna shook her head, staring at the floor.
"No," she whispered.*

*Suddenly Papa's hand was on her, pushing
her up against the wall, his fingers gripping her
chin tightly. She let out a cry of pain and tried to
pry his fingers off, unsuccessfully. "You better not
be thinkin' that. I already lost my wife, I don't need
to lose you too."*

*Adranna instinctively shut her eyes, trying to
calm herself. She had quickly learned that showing
her fear just angered her father more — better to
put up a mask and ride out the wave of anger than
to give him more fuel to continue.*

*She took a deep breath and opened her eyes.
Glancing up, she gasped... Papa's eyes were not
bloodshot; they were red. Blood red irises, bulging
and angry.*

*He tilted his head, looking down at her
thoughtfully. "Your mother chose you," he said
slowly, his tightening grip causing her to cry out
involuntarily. "She wanted a child. She wanted
someone to look after... I didn't. She said it would help
us." He made a face, and to Adranna's surprise, his
eyes welled up with tears. "Lot of help it did, now she's*

dead. But now that I've got you, you ain't goin' anywhere."

He let go abruptly, then, staring down at his hands in bewilderment. Adranna quickly touched where Papa had gripped her, wincing, grateful that this was where he had chosen to stop, as he turned and stumbled away, muttering to himself.

That night Adranna slipped into the forest and escaped from the Northern Village, hoping that she had seen the last of those red eyes.

♦

Marie pushed through the crowd of people that had formed. She reached the source of commotion: Chancellor was muttering quietly to a pacing and very aggravated Wyatt, who ignored his requests and contributed his own much louder mutterings.

"I saw it with my own eyes! It was like a specter, with the claws and the eyes, and the... the kind of glow they have... but it was bigger. And meaner! Much meaner. Looking, anyway..."

Marie approached Chancellor, who looked impatient. She noted the wounds peppering Wyatt's skin. "We need to get him to the bathhouse."

Chancellor shook his head. "We've been trying. He's been doing this for half an hour and he hasn't lost any steam yet."

He reached forward and grabbed Wyatt's arm, but Wyatt wrenched free, taking a step backward. "No! NO! You've got to listen to me!" His face reddened, and he took a deep breath, focusing now on Marie's fresh ears. "I saw down there! It's like another world! And that thing…" He shivered. "…It came along and it opened its mouth, and it screamed at me! And it lunged towards me, and… if they hadn't pulled me up, I would probably be floating around under there, torn to shreds!"

The crowd of onlookers exchanged apprehensive glances — the boy was already pretty torn up as it was. Marie shot a look at Chancellor, and gently took hold of Wyatt's elbow. "All right, Wyatt, let's just get you cleaned up—"

Wyatt wrenched his arm away again. "No! That thing, whatever it is, is angry at us! Like… like the fact that we're taking bodies from the mud infuriates it. I… I…"

He pressed the palms of his hands into his eyelids, wilting. Chancellor gave a nervous glance at the crowd of people, which was buzzing with fearful excitement. "Come on, son. Let's get you some rest."

Wyatt succumbed and allowed Chancellor to take him away.

Once the boy had been cleaned up, his wounds bandaged, he was taken to the Guest House, where he almost immediately lost consciousness, his body eager to restore itself in a deep sleep.

Marie, Mama Nina, and Chancellor met in the otherwise empty Guest House, calling a meeting in order. They stared at Wyatt, each engrossed in their own thoughts. "I would like to hear him describe this monster," Mama said finally.

"He told us it looked like a specter," Marie said, glad for the distraction of the patch she was sewing on an article of clothing. She was having a hard time looking at the boy without feeling a strange sense of dread.

"But I would like to hear it myself," Mama said. "I can't judge how much he believes his own words without looking him in the face while he says them."

"Well," Chancellor offered, "they patched him up well."

"Why was there even need to patch him up in the first place?"

"They've attacked before."

Marie shook her head. "Never four at once."

"Maybe they didn't get their lunch today."

Marie dropped her sewing roughly to the side, giving Chancellor a cold look. He cleared his throat uncomfortably.

Mama cleared the air. "What are we to do with him once he awakens?"

"We'll send him back home in the morning." Marie turned to Chancellor. "I assume you've reached that conclusion as well."

"I think that would be best, yes," Chancellor said, nodding. "Get him away from the point of trauma."

"And what if he is telling the truth?"

Marie glanced in surprise at Mama, who avoided her gaze, staring down at her lap. "I don't doubt that he's telling the truth," Marie replied. "He very well does believe he saw what he saw. But he's in shock... specters under the mud? It's absurd. He's confused, is all."

"Now, wait a minute," Chancellor said, holding up a hand. "Marie... do you remember the conversations we've had about newcomers having nightmares for weeks after surfacing?"

Marie stared at him, a sinking feeling in the pit of her stomach. "Yes."

Mama Nina let out an odd puff of air. "No one ever remembers what happens in the nightmares," she said.

Marie squinted at her, puzzled at her composure, then turned to Chancellor in rebuttal. "They're stress dreams, being in a new environment," she protested. "There's nothing to prove that they dreamed of a specter under the mud."

Chancellor shrugged; he could not deny the lack of evidence. But Mama Nina gave a miserable sigh. "I would believe they were stress dreams if they happened consistently," she said quietly. "Most who had those dreams surfaced years ago... but you've said yourself, Marie, that the children have been having nightmares recently. Every single child who surfaced in the last few years."

Wyatt stirred in his sleep, mumbling something. Chancellor rushed to the side of the bed, kneeling, but he didn't say anything

131

more. He glanced back at Marie, a worried look etched on his face. "She has a point, Marie," he said quietly. "I don't remember a damn thing about those dreams… not a single image. But I remember being terrified of them all the same. If there is something under there that's causing these dreams, then maybe we ought to stop making small news about when people fall under."

"So what, are you saying this has happened before?"

"I don't know, Marie. But clearly there is something new under the mud that is terrifying children. Perhaps it is this specter that the boy speaks of."

Marie stared at Wyatt, now unable to *not* look at him. She cleared her throat. "There's plenty to be scared about under the fields other than a silly figment of our imagination. But that's beside the point. There's nothing under there but bodies," she said confidently, though a little less confident than she was to start off.

♦

Paul sat beside Wyatt's bedside, watching John pace around the room. The two men were not sure what to say to each other, and both secretly hoped that the sleeping boy would awaken soon and end the awkward silence. It was John's sixth time around the room, absentmindedly tapping each bed as he made his round, though quietly enough not to waken the inhabitants of the beds.

Paul examined Wyatt's face as he slept. His eyes rolled back and forth under his eyelids, his mouth twitching. Paul idly wondered if he was having a good dream or a bad dream. He could only hope it was a good dream, seeing as how he was going to get bad news upon awakening.

He had to give him credit: here was a boy who pushed all the rules of society aside, and interacted with all people as if they were decent, regardless of whether they were or weren't. While anyone else would find relief in the fact that they had an excuse to return home, Wyatt would actually be upset to learn that he was being sent away from his new friends, as he saw them — sent away from an opportunity to help. Paul smiled. Wyatt's innocence may be exhausting, but Paul couldn't help but hold some affection toward the boy; his enthusiasm made the load of life seem just a little lighter.

Wyatt began to stir, a small cry escaping his lips, and his eyes opened. Quickly, John dropped his tapping game and rushed to Wyatt's bedside. "Good morning!"

Wyatt lifted his head and drowsily made eye contact with John. "Where am I?"

"You're in the Guest House."

Wyatt touched his bandages gingerly; Paul could practically see the memories of the day before flooding back into his mind.

John tousled what little of Wyatt's hair was not pinned down by the bandages. "Take it easy, kiddo. You got your ass kicked by those specters."

Wyatt glanced over at Paul. "I bet you were glad to have your house back again last night."

Paul smiled slowly. "It *was* strange to sleep without the sound of snoring coming from the other room."

Wyatt made an attempt at a grin. "Well, you better not get used to it. I'll be back soon enough."

Paul quickly turned his gaze to John, clearing his throat pointedly. John nodded and stepped in. "Actually, Wyatt, you're a lucky one. You get to go home."

Wyatt stared at him, the information not quite clicking. "Go home?"

The look on his face wracked Paul with guilt. He feebly held up the knapsack that sat at his feet. "I've put together some provisions for your trip."

Wyatt was silent for a moment. He narrowed his eyes. "...What? I can't go home!"

"Sheriff's orders."

Wyatt sprang up, pushing his blanket to the floor. "She's not *my* sheriff..."

Paul stood, not really in an effort to stop him, but mostly in an effort to seem like he was stopping him — he was actually looking forward to seeing the boy make a stand. John, on the other hand, quickly followed him out of the Guest House. Paul watched as he chased Wyatt to the corner of the field that Marie patrolled. He couldn't help but smile at the look of apprehension that crossed her face as they reached her.

From afar he watched them speak, Wyatt becoming more and more distressed as Marie remained a relentless fortress. She placed a hand gently on his shoulder, and she and John led him back to the Guest House.

"You were attacked by four specters yesterday, Mr. Pine," Marie was saying as they came within earshot. "I thought you'd be grateful for the opportunity—"

"I can't leave now!" Wyatt sighed. "Not after what I've seen under your field, I need to—"

John scowled. "You need to what, Wyatt? Get rid of it? Are you going to dive on in and take care of that yourself?"

Wyatt narrowed his eyes. "Well, no, but—"

"Then I suggest you go home and get some rest where you'll have your family to look to you." Marie nudged Wyatt toward the door of the Guest House.

"How old are you, Wyatt?" Paul asked suddenly. All eyes turned on him.

"Seventeen," Wyatt said, a perplexed look on his face.

Paul turned to Marie. "No offense, Sheriff, but the boy's old enough to make his own decisions," he stated simply. "If he wants to stay, maybe you should let him stay."

Marie raised an eyebrow. "And no offense to you, Paul, but this really isn't any of your business. As the Sheriff, I have every right to make this call."

Paul held Marie's gaze for a moment, then nodded. Wyatt gave him an appreciative smile, which Paul returned. He held open the door to the Guest House, motioning for Wyatt to enter, but the boy did not budge.

Chancellor approached from the field. He eyed the group warily, then focused in on Wyatt; Paul guessed with amusement that he was trying to gauge the intensity of the situation by the shade of red that Wyatt's face had taken on.

"Chancellor," said Marie as he reached them, "you can escort him back to the Western Village after he gets some breakfast in him."

Chancellor blinked at her. Clearly he wasn't going anywhere. John sighed and stepped forward. "I'll bring him back. And I'll return by lunch time to continue digging."

Marie nodded. "Good." She made her departure, walking back in the direction of the field.

"This is so stupid!" Wyatt yelled, kicking at the wall of the Guest House. Paul quickly closed the door to block the noise from waking the children.

Chancellor placed a hand on Wyatt's shoulder comfortingly. "I'm sorry, Wyatt. I shouldn't have allowed such a young digger to come in the first place."

"I'm not lying about the specter, Sheriff," Wyatt pleaded. "I mean, I wouldn't even call it a specter, I'd call it a... a beast! I don't understand why everyone is so quick to ignore a threat to their field. And besides, I came to help dig! Beast or not, I still have to stay to help you find your daughter."

John cleared his throat. "Sheriff, maybe we should talk about that possibly not happening, as well."

Chancellor dropped his hand to his side, his eyes glazing over. He began to walk away.

"Sheriff!" John yelled after him. He sighed, and turned back to Wyatt. "Personally, I'd love to trade places with you, Wyatt. You get to go home. Show some appreciation."

He took off after Chancellor. Wyatt turned to Paul, sighing. "Thanks for trying," he said, taking the knapsack from Paul and entering the Guest House with a miserable look upon his face.

Paul shook his head. This day was already off to an excellent start.

♦

Mukisa slid one of her knives into her belt and hopped out her front door. She was running a little late; the other hunters were probably waiting for her at the edge of the forest.

She started walking in that direction, but stopped short when she heard hushed voices inside the Guest House.

"What exactly did you see?"

For some reason this caught Mukisa off guard. That sounded like a private conversation;

she glanced around and saw children running and laughing on the green. So they had been kicked out of bed and shooed out of the Guest House.

Mukisa frowned and crept over to the window, slyly peeking through. Inside, Mama Nina and Wyatt sat facing each other, Mama Nina in her overgrown robe, her hands folded neatly on her lap, and Wyatt wrapped in bandages nearly head to toe. Marie and Chancellor lurked in the corner of the room, watching.

"What exactly did you see?" Mama Nina prompted again, giving Wyatt a soothing smile, the wrinkles nearly folding over her eyes.

Wyatt fidgeted with the hem of his shirt, avoiding eye contact. Mukisa glanced at the stool before him and noted the plate of untouched biscuits that someone had gifted him as a way of calming his nerves. They must be questioning him about the attack.

"I saw what you see flying above your village," Wyatt replied slowly, glancing out at the sky through the window (Mukisa ducked down, swearing under her breath) with a touch of worry on his face. "Glowing, winged, with talons... except bigger. Head honcho size."

"Is there any distinguishing factor other than the difference in size?"

Wyatt thought for a moment. "I can't remember," he whispered weakly.

Mama leaned forward and placed a weathered hand over his. "Take a moment to try."

Wyatt closed his eyes, and almost instantly, fear etched across his face, as if the specter had revisited him underneath the cover of his eyelids. He stayed that way for several moments, shivering in the heat.

Mukisa couldn't help but cringe; the fearful look on Wyatt's face was almost enough to make her walk away right then, and find distraction in the hunt she was supposed to be getting to. But suddenly Wyatt's eyes shot open. He looked up at Mama Nina, and swallowed hard. "The eyes," he whispered. "The eyes were different. The specters, they have that blueish glow to them, everything is that whiteish-blue, including their eyes. This one was just like that, except its eyes glowed red."

Mukisa felt the hair on the back of her neck stand straight up. She glanced at her parents in the corner, and saw that they were having similar reactions: her mother was putting up her mask again, struggling to keep her emotions in check, and Chancellor deftly directed his gaze to the ground.

Mama Nina's reaction was more disconcerting. She had a look of defeat on her face — a strange, kind of conflicted defeat, as if she had just won a bet, but had been hoping that she would lose. She nodded slowly. "Tell me, child… why would there be a specter under the mud?"

Wyatt's look could have burned a hole right through the wall. "Why does no one believe me? I'm not lying to you, I—"

"Child, I'm not saying I don't believe you," Mama said. "I would just like to hear your reasoning."

Wyatt nodded, staring at the ground. He shrugged. "Maybe it's been under there for a while... but we're just now seeing the signs."

Mama was silent for a moment, staring morosely at her hands, folded neatly in her lap. She seemed to be trying to make a decision. Finally she stood and turned to the nervous spectators. "This boy needs to stay in the Southern Village," she stated simply, moving toward the door. "And what's more, we need to listen to him. At least give him a trial before the people."

Mukisa's eyes widened. Across the room, her mother looked startled. "Why?"

Mama Nina stopped at the door, gazing intently at Wyatt with a look of empathy splayed across her face. "Because I remember my nightmares," she said. "And Wyatt just described them exactly."

And with that she was out the door. Mukisa stumbled backwards, trying to remain hidden, but Mama Nina caught sight of her, gave her a despondent nod, and continued walking. Her heart seemed heavy with distraction as she ambled away.

♦

They had pulled the benches out, but no one bothered to sit; instead, they stood in clumps around the village square, arguing fearfully amongst themselves. Mukisa watched her mother standing at the front of the assembly, urging people to take a seat, but by the time they complied, the meeting could have been going on for twenty minutes already.

She couldn't blame them for being so riled up — news traveled fast in the Southern Village. She was still unnerved by what she had heard in the Guest House. She didn't necessarily want to believe that what the boy said was true, but it was like the ghost stories that Mama Nina would occasionally tell at celebrations: you would laugh at them in front of the other listeners, but as soon as you were given time to dwell on the subject, the details of the story would seep into your mind, and take hold of your every thought. Mukisa always relished those stories; but in this case, she was not ready to embrace the red eyes from Wyatt's encounter. She didn't understand... why red eyes? The sight of Martin's red eyes flashed in her mind, and she shivered.

Mukisa sat nervously next to Paul, unable to sit still. The village was not used to having so many town meetings in one week, and while Marie had rejected the idea of giving Wyatt a trial — no seventeen year old should have to go through an entire village picking him apart if he didn't have to — she had at least recognized that she had to address the village somehow. Mukisa had an uneasy feeling about what her mother's line of action was going to be for this particular situation.

"All right, everyone," her mother announced wearily, staring out at the assembly. "There has been a..." She cleared her throat. "A *development* with the situation in the field."

"What's down there?" a villager called out.

Marie frowned. "I urge you all that there is no reason to panic... but it seems that a specter has been spotted under the mud."

"How is that not a reason to panic?!" someone called out, and the crowd buzzed in agreement.

Marie held up her hands to quiet them. "Only one person has seen the specter recently... but we have reason to believe that others may have seen it at some point, years ago. And for now, that's enough that I feel inclined to do something about it. So, whatever it is that's under there, we're going to give it some space. There will be no digging for the next two weeks."

Mukisa flinched, unable to disguise the shock that went rippling through her body. Two weeks?! She had expected there to be a ban on the field, but in her mind a reasonable time frame would have been a day, maybe two. Two weeks was... well, it was two weeks longer that Cecilia would be stuck under that mud.

Around her, the villagers exchanged glances, sharing in Mukisa's disbelief. Her father, especially, seemed to be in shock about the statement.

Marie cleared her throat. "As most of you know, this is a very hard decision for me to make, in light of..." Her mask flickered for a moment, then steadied. "...situations. I acknowledge that there are people under there who need our help."

There was a moment's pause as she stared out at the crowd of whispering villagers. Mukisa caught her mother's eye. For a moment, she thought that for once, the look of wide eyed outrage on her face might change her mother's mind. But Marie continued, a tinge of sadness in her voice. "And they'll still be there in two weeks."

This was almost too much for Mukisa to take. Her face hardened to an element sturdier than steel. She made a move to stand, and Paul gently stuck his hand out, clasping her arm and easing her back into her seat.

"Heart of stone, Sheriff!" a villager yelled out, reflecting Mukisa's mood, and a few people booed.

"This is not an easy decision! But I won't have another villager fall under because I didn't take any measures."

"But no digging means no celebration!"

An outcry ripped through the crowd.

"Newcomers have been sparse these past few weeks. And we've had a celebration every month for the last — well — we've never *not* had a celebration!"

Mama Nina stood slowly from the midst of the assembly, shaking her head. "Just because we don't have any newcomers doesn't mean there isn't a reason for us to celebrate."

No one looked convinced.

Mukisa stood abruptly, pushing Paul's hands aside. "Hold on. One person has seen something! One! And he's from the *Western Village*..." (Wyatt heaved a heavy sigh from the corner) "Why should we trust *him*?"

She scanned the assembly, breathing heavily, silently daring the crowd to stop their whispering and stand with her. Paul stared up at her, shocked.

But Mukisa could see that her mother was not shocked. She locked eyes with her and saw the look of understanding in her face: she would recognize that her outburst was more out of fear than of anger. She would understand how terrified Mukisa was that Wyatt might be right, because she, herself, shared that fear. Because if he *was* right — and Mukisa was all for this idea to be proven wrong — but if he *was* right, then Cecilia was in more danger than just being lost to the field. The fact that there was a threat amidst the mud strengthened her resolve even more. She wanted people to dig.

The rest of the village, however, was much more inclined to superficial thinking. Mukisa knew exactly what they were whispering to one another: why *should* we trust him? He's not one of *us*.

From the corner, Wyatt stood meekly,

and shuffled toward the head of the assembly. Marie gave him a wary look, but let him come forward. The scathing looks from the surrounding company did not lessen, but the whispers did.

Wyatt cleared his throat.

"I know," he began, "that you don't want to trust me. Fine... then don't. Even though I've been digging with your crew for almost a week now. And even though I've never shown any tendency of violence or deceit or—" He swallowed, realizing that his words were not exactly soothing the crowd. "What I mean is, I know it's hard to believe what I saw under the mud. But let me assure you, whether you believe something or not, it still could very well be true, so shame on you for not wanting to take precautions. But..." He glanced over at Marie, his look one of indecision and guilt, and suddenly, with a burst of hope, Mukisa knew exactly where this was headed. "But putting up a ban just won't cut it — ignoring it doesn't mean it will ignore you. We need to take action! So leave the field alone for a couple weeks... it won't do you any harm. But in a couple weeks, you'll go back on that field, and the threat to your safety will still exist! It will still be there, lurking under the field, masking itself in the security of your village's womb — a place out of which life is born, and there's a hungry devil underneath. So please be aware, eventually you're going to have to deal with the beast itself."

A murmur ran through the crowd as he returned to his seat. Mukisa glanced around, feeling slightly victorious. Perhaps something good would come of this; perhaps it was finally okay that the village was so easily swayed by their fear. Maybe they would fight back; maybe they would contest the ban.

But that just wasn't going to happen, was it? No, she thought, as the meeting adjourned, the ban still firmly in place... Wyatt's words would not inspire anyone to action. Even if the village began to argue, they would argue themselves right back into stagnation.

Well, then Mukisa would just have to stir the pot. If no one else was willing to dig, then she would do it. She had already made up her mind — she didn't care if the ban was in place, it didn't matter. She would dig to find Cecilia, and she would keep digging until she was found. She just wouldn't do it in sight of her mother.

But there was something that continued to nag at the back of Mukisa's mind, and it took her a few days to put her finger on exactly what it was. Mama Nina's words kept pushing their way into her conscience. *Because I remember my nightmares...*

But no one remembered their nightmares; and Mama Nina had never mentioned that she was any different. How many times had Mukisa overheard her mother talking to the old woman about the nightmares that the children had, heard them commiserating over the faceless dreams and the lack of control that they had over them?

So was Mama Nina lying, trying to back Wyatt up? Or had she been lying before, to cover up her memories? She didn't seem to have any motive to so adamantly support a citizen from the Western Village.

She found Mama Nina in front of her house one night at dinner time, stooping forward to stoke a fire. She hadn't even realized she had gone looking for her; but here she was — as usual, her feet had made the trip for her — and, well, if she was already here, she might as well ask the woman what was on her mind.

She sat beside Mama Nina, avoiding eye contact. Mama smiled, a knowing smile, and for a moment neither of them said a word. She already knows why I'm here, thought Mukisa, frowning. Or — and this was not an option to be ruled out — she simply always had that knowing smile on her face, making it appear that she knew. Maybe she just pretended to know everything, until she had picked up enough clues to figure out through the context of a matter. Mukisa smiled inwardly at the thought.

"You want to know why I never told anyone of my nightmares."

So she *did* know. The words were said with such certainty that Mukisa felt that she had read her mind. She nodded. "I'd say it's a fair curiosity."

Mama Nina smiled. "You and your mother are just alike. She came to me just yesterday, after the same information. And do you know what I told her?"

"What?"

The wind shifted, wafting the smoke from the fire right into Mama Nina's face. She barely batted an eye. The look on her face was distant; with all that smoke and mystery billowing around her, she looked like a mystic from those stories that Mukisa used to pry out of her mother at bedtime. "That I didn't tell anyone because I was afraid," Mama said slowly, thoughtfully.

"What, of the specter?"

Mama Nina chuckled, glancing quickly at her in amusement. "If only," she replied. Mukisa wondered at this, but had no time to dwell, for the old woman continued. "When I was younger, when I first started having the nightmares, it took me a while to piece together that many of my friends also had them. But then it began to dawn on me… everyone else's nightmares were faceless. For whatever reason, my nightmares set me apart from the others. Now, to most people, being set apart may not be so horrible… but I was shy, and I didn't like attention on me, and so I never told a soul.

"Mukisa, many years have passed since those days. I have watched many people struggle over their memories of the field, of the dreams that haunted them without ever showing their face. I also watched, with relief, as those nightmares suddenly seemed to clear up, and the newcomers were smiling and rosy-cheeked when they awoke. And do you know what? I eventually began to realize that if I ever did tell people of my dreams, it would frighten them. Make them fear going out on the field to dig. *Make them actually believe a monster was under the mud."*

"So you kept it from us to keep us from worrying."

"Well, after a time, I had gotten used to keeping my secrets. That's the nice part about being old... you don't have to explain why you're doing something after a while. People simply attribute it to the methods of a creature of habit. But yes... I suppose that reasoning has carried with me, until now."

"And you think... you think Wyatt was right? Maybe he just remembered his own nightmares and absorbed the images into his memories."

Mama Nina frowned, and Mukisa could tell she was holding something on the tip of her tongue. She sighed. "If that's the case, then that means that we do, in fact, have the same nightmares. Living in different villages, too! Which begs the question..."

Mukisa furrowed her brow, thinking. She remembered her father telling her when she was a child that he had nightmares when he was growing up, years after he had surfaced from the field. And that had been all the way over in the Western Village.

But Mama Nina clapped her hands. "But that's silly, isn't it? Truth is, this is an isolated incident. Isn't it? A rarity. Otherwise it would have happened before."

Mukisa glanced sidelong at her. There she was, holding back secrets again. But she supposed, now, she had her own secrets to keep. She wondered if she should mention her run-in with Martin before his fall; she wondered if she should mention his eyes. But no… he had probably just been crying. She had mistaken his grief for something more menacing. She shrugged off the thought, and focused on her worry. "So there is something down there, then."

"Trust me," Mama said gently, "I don't want there to be anything down there any more than you do. But we have facts placed in front of us, and to disregard the facts would be to betray the people of this village. Put them in danger."

"Yes, but how did it get there? And why?"

Mama was silent for a moment. "Child," she said slowly, "there are things that you will never understand. And that may not be a bad thing. Sometimes our knowledge protects us; and sometimes it destroys us."

Mukisa did not like the way that sounded. "What do you mean?"

The old woman sighed. "What I mean is, we need to focus on other questions. Questions such as… How do we fix this? How do we remove the danger?"

Mukisa grimaced. "Mama answered that question by putting a ban on the field."

Mama Nina gave her an imploring look. "Do you think so? I don't see that as an answer, really… more of a desperate move to buy more time. Your mother is scared, Mukisa. She's never dealt with this situation before, nor has anyone in this village."

Mukisa chewed on her lip for a moment. She wouldn't deny Mama Nina's words, but she still wished her mother had come up with another way to stall for time.

Mama Nina tilted her head thoughtfully. "I find I disagree with the ban. It simply leaves little Cecilia and all the other trapped souls to fend for themselves, hmm?" She shook her head. "No, there must be another way to deal with the beast under the field."

"What are you suggesting?"

The question came from behind Mukisa. She turned to see her mother standing just on the edge of the firelight, regarding them with a defeated look on her face. "Please," she said, "if you have any ideas, let me know. Because I've been trying to figure out what to do ever since we had that damned town meeting."

Mama Nina looked at her, surprised. "I'm not suggesting anything. I'm just telling you there must be another way."

Marie gave a small smile, joining them by the fire. "I suppose we could ask Wyatt his opinion on the matter."

"Why would we ask him?" Mukisa retorted, and her mother sent her a harsh look. She sent it right back.

Mama raised an eyebrow. "Now, the boy may have insight, but I wouldn't give him the responsibility of naming our next move."

"Well, I'm not about to call another town meeting," Marie sighed. "The more I call, the antsier the village gets."

"Suppose you ask Chancellor?"

Marie gave Mama Nina an exhausted look. "It always comes back to asking him, doesn't it?"

Mama placed her hand gently on Marie's cheek, smiling. "I'm not saying he is the authority on the situation, dear. And I recognize that the way the Western Villagers treat him as such has been weighing on you." Marie frowned. "But we need to be creative about what we are to do, and perhaps an outside opinion would be helpful. Perhaps we should ask him what the Western Village would do."

Marie shook her head sternly. "Mama, I know this is not the mature thing to say, but at this moment I don't give a damn what the Western Village would do."

Mukisa chose this moment to extricate herself from the conversation. It was turning into a meeting of the village elders, and though she normally loved to hear what happened behind closed doors in the village, the look on her mother's face told her she needed a moment of privacy with her wise-woman.

The whole situation was infuriating. Everyone recognized that the village had a problem, but no one had any idea what they should do about it. Typical. She at least agreed with her mother on one account: this was not a matter for her father to get his hands on. It may take some thinking, but surely they could come up with an idea that didn't include asking for help from foreigners. She knew what a mess that could be.

8

The Talk

Wyatt sat beside a basin of water, scrubbing his fingers. It was useless: the grime remained, caked underneath his nails. It was the only reason he regretted staying in the Southern Village after his incident on the field — yes, he wanted to stay and help fight the specter in any way he could, but he also missed not being mud-stained. It was the little things: the Southies had become very adept at cleaning underneath their nails, but the Western Village was so used to shovels that... well, Wyatt hadn't even been on the field in four days, and there were still traces of it on his body. He, Chancellor, and John had been assigned to the garden, which was dirtying to some extent, but called more for stooping and picking the ripe vegetables than it did kneeling in deep mud... no, this dirt that plagued him was from the field.

"Got enough water there to take a bath." John sat beside him, scooping up a handful of water for himself and rinsing his hands. "Maybe next time don't pour yourself so much."

Wyatt frowned. "It's so easy to forget how rare water is around these parts." But not *too* easy to forget, he thought, examining the dirt under his nails wistfully.

John leaned back and squinted at the sun. "Yeah, I guess we're lucky in that respect."

"To have to walk so far just to get a few jugs of water is kind of ridiculous, don't you think?"

John turned his squinty gaze on Wyatt. "Well, when it's the only option..."

Wyatt gave him a look. "It is very clearly not the only option, John."

He laughed, more of a warning than an impulse. "What are you, on their side now?"

Wyatt shook his head, sighing. "What is it with the sides, John? Why are you so against the Southern Village?"

John sighed and rubbed the sweat off his brow with the back of his hand. He was silent for a moment before answering. "It's not that I'm against the Southern Village, Wyatt. It's just that we're very different people. We have different ways. There was a time when we all held the same values, and went about life in the same way... but... I don't know, I guess that's what separation does to you over time. They started doing things differently." He smirked. "And then they started getting all self-righteous because we started changing things for the better." Wyatt smiled in spite of himself, knowing John was thinking about the shovels. "But just because a way of life isn't exactly what it was 50 years ago, doesn't mean it's wrong. If anything, it means we're improving the system. We're not outdated."

"I don't know. Just because a way of life is old, doesn't mean it's outdated. It's kind of nice to see people staying true to their roots."

"You really have gone to their side." John laughed. "All right, I guess there's not anything *wrong* with being old-fashioned. But the way they do things... it sets us apart."

"But why does the way we do things make us better than anybody—?"

"I didn't say better."

Wyatt gave him a challenging look. "Okay, what? Just smarter, more deserving of privileges..."

"Wyatt, that's just the way life is." John thought for a moment. "Do you remember a few years ago, when there was that whole to-do with the Northern Village?" Wyatt shook his head. "Of course not, you weren't even a teenager yet, you had your head in the clouds. Well, someone had run away from the Northern Village, and ended up here, in the Southern Village. For years. Some kind of abuse going on that made the girl run. Anyway, the point was, for years the Northern Village assumed that the girl had gotten herself lost in the wilderness and died."

"Who was it?" Wyatt asked.

John shrugged. "They kept it all hush hush, didn't care to tell any of us the details... we heard most of 'em, anyway, but not that. Anyway, then they caught whiff of the girl being here... and they sent people to look for her. But this girl had already set up fort in the village, and adopted customs and such..." John leaned in, trying not to let his voice carry too far. "So the people of the Southern Village went up in arms to keep this girl under their care... basically started a small civil war between the villages, from what I can tell, and just... I mean, someone died. That's how ridiculous it was. See, you grew up in a peaceful village, Wyatt, so you don't understand... outside of the Western Village, people just snap. They cling to their outdated ways and they don't learn how to adapt; and when someone comes along and tests them, they snap. That's how violence happens."

Wyatt frowned. "But you said she ran because of abuse. So the Southern Village was trying to protect her."

John shook his head. "There are other ways of protection. If it had been the Western Village, we would've handled it much differently."

"How do you think we would've handled Martin?"

John stared blankly at him. "What do you mean?"

Wyatt furrowed his brow, embarrassed. "I mean... do you think we could have prevented him from going out onto the field?"

"With all the crazy shit that happens in this village? Sometimes there's nothing we can do to stop a thing from happening, Wyatt. Even if we did stop him, he would have gone out there at some other time."

Wyatt buried his head in his arms. "But why would he do it?"

John gave him an affectionate squeeze on the shoulder. "You gotta stop caring so much about people you don't know, kiddo. Martin was some kind of sick. It's probably best that he gets more time with Mother Mud — nobody else was gonna be able to help him."

Wyatt lifted his head to show tears streaming down his cheeks. "I beg to differ."

John sighed and shook his head. "Differ away then, Wyatt. Do what you like. But it doesn't change what's happened."

"He's down there... just floating around."

John stared at Wyatt, suddenly understanding his tears. "Is that what you saw underneath the mud?" he asked softly.

Wyatt nodded, avoiding eye contact. "There were so many of them. Looked like they were..." He trailed off for a moment, looking away; he couldn't bring himself to say it. "...Asleep."

John pictured the scene and felt the hair on the back of his neck rise. "Well, you know what's true, Wyatt," he said softly. "The field's got them in its care. They're alive, and just waiting for us to pull them back up."

"After who knows how long. And until then, they're just floating, and time goes on without them. And now with the specter... we have no idea what it's capable of doing under there!" Wyatt sighed. "I'm not just gonna stop caring so much about people I don't know. 'Cause I know 'em well enough to know they don't deserve that."

John had no words. He watched as Wyatt got up and stumbled away, wiping his eyes; then he lashed out and pushed the basin of water beside him, watching the water slosh over the sides and into the grass.

♦

Mukisa eased the door to her house closed, ever so gently. The darkness pressed in on her, making her grateful for the sparse pricks of light from the fireflies scattered about; she grabbed a lantern that had been left out in the open, carefully lit it, and crept over to the field.

She reached the edge of the field, and a noise grabbed her attention. Whirling around, her first glance was back at the Guest House — had to make sure she hadn't woken Mama. Her eyes swept over the village green, the forest…

Satisfied with the return of silence, she stepped out onto the field, her toes sinking slightly into the mud, and made her way toward the center. And she began to dig.

Digging at night went, quite frankly, against everything Mukisa's mother had taught her. First, for the simple fact that you couldn't trust your judgment in the dark: how far were you reaching into the mud? How active was the field at any given moment? You really couldn't tell. Second, for the fact that there were no others to help you if you began to fall. Mukisa glanced up at the night sky. Though she couldn't see the specters, she couldn't say whether they were sleeping or lurking just out of sight in the forest. Did specters sleep? She shuddered, and kept digging.

There was something unnerving about digging at all. For years, she had avoided the field — she had never had the defiant attitude that Cecilia had had, flying in the face of the villagers' reservations about a bastard digging on holy ground. And especially with Mukisa's history, she had always felt it better to leave that particular fight alone. Now that she was out here, she was sure the field would have some objection to her hands taking liberties in its soil.

Another noise made her jump. She quickly scanned the area, her heart rate spiking. There was movement by the square.

She squinted, and her heart dropped into her stomach as she realized it was the figure of a man.

She stood. "Show yourself," she challenged, hoping that her voice wouldn't carry too much further past the figure.

The figure sighed and stepped into the light of her lantern. She rolled her eyes; it was her father. He walked out onto the field, gave her an apologetic look, and knelt beside her, starting to dig.

Mukisa tried to decide which tactic to use to revile him. At a loss, she finally settled with "I was here first," lifting her chin in the air stubbornly.

"Mukisa, I've been coming out here every night for the past three weeks. Don't tell me you were here first."

Mukisa narrowed her eyes, set down the lantern, and plopped down in the mud beside him. The suddenness of her movement made him jump. "Don't be so careless!" he cried.

"If you're going to lecture me, you can just go back to the Western Village *right now*." As if to punctuate her words, she picked up a handful of mud and slung it out at the rest of the field.

Chancellor stared at his daughter, marveling at her obstinance. "You know, as much as it may pain you to realize, I actually don't want my own daughter to fall under. I already suffered through that once. I don't want you both gone."

Mukisa let these words sink in for a moment. She hated that she couldn't argue with him on that point. It would be so much easier if she could. She slung another handful of mud away from her work in defiance. "So what *do* you want?"

He glanced at her, surprised. "I want a truce."

Mukisa rolled her eyes. "Listen to yourself."

"Look, I'm trying to fix what I've done. I know that you would've liked to have had me around—"

"Don't go and make yourself think you're wanted," Mukisa said, raising her chin in defiance.

Chancellor sighed. "I'm trying to make up for walking out on my family. But there's only so much I can do. You can be mad at me... hell, you can hate me. But at least talk to me."

"I'm talking to you now."

"No, Mukisa, you're berating me. That's not the same thing."

Mukisa suddenly spun around, and turned her back on him, digging another portion of the mud. She had intended for it to be rude, shutting him out as she worked, but she realized as her body halted that that wasn't it. There was a tension in her body, and it wasn't her usual annoyance or anger that had sent her in another direction: she was starting to cry. The tears felt hot on her cheeks, and she closed her eyes, trying to steady her breathing, blindly working her hands through the mud in an attempt to ignore this sudden onslaught of emotion.

Behind her, Chancellor sat patiently, silently. That damn man was going to wait her out. She swallowed, finding her voice. "When I was little," she said slowly, "Mama told me that Cecilia and I were special. We weren't just pulled from the mud... we were brought to this community by a force much greater than strength."

She reached down and combed her hand through the mud halfheartedly, and wondered if she was done talking; but the pit in her stomach said otherwise. Her mouth opened and more words tumbled out. "It took me a while to realize that maybe she was spinning the truth a little. There was another definition of 'special' that meant an oddity — a disgrace. I've been alive for nineteen years, and I somehow evaded the mud! The village cries 'heretic' every day." She was faintly aware that she had stopped digging now; she was just sitting there in the mud, in the dark. "And then you add insult to injury, and you just leave?"

The silence behind her was killing her. But after a moment, there came a weak reply: "I had responsibilities. I was asked to lead the Western Village. You knew that — you and your mother both knew that."

Mukisa turned on him, no longer bothering to hide the angry tears in her eyes. "But you didn't have to do it. You could have stayed here, and raised Cecilia. Been here to watch me get betrothed. You could have stayed here with Mama. Comforted her after all the hell she went through. That *we* went through." She took a deep, jagged breath. "You didn't leave because you wanted to be Sheriff. And you didn't even leave because you were ashamed of your goddamned bastard daughters. You left because of what I did!"

She hadn't completely realized that she believed that until the words came out of her mouth. Chancellor stared at her, his eyes wide, and Mukisa let her glare wither; she stared down at the mud, all the energy sapped from her body. This time when she spoke, it was less out of anger and more out of exhaustion. "All right. You got your wish. I talked to you. Now can I go?"

Chancellor nodded, still speechless, and Mukisa picked herself up and walked away, her sight once more becoming blurry with tears. She couldn't stop the memories from bombarding her, memories that she had done so well at forgetting up until this moment… and now, closing her eyes, she could picture the scene very clearly: coming back from hunting, the carcass of her latest kill slung over one shoulder, she noticed the crowd of villagers standing by the Guest House and approached curiously. She remembered hearing voices: angry voices, some of them familiar. But she couldn't see beyond the wall of people.

"I hear you've been breeding with my daughter," an unfamiliar voice was saying. A man's voice, gruff and deep.

"I have a relationship with her. She is not an animal." This voice belonged to her father.

There came a curt laugh from the unfamiliar voice. "Clearly you don't know my Adranna."

She heard the door to the Guest House slam open, and caught a glimpse of her mother glaring down into the crowd. Presumably at the unfamiliar voice. "Don't call me by that name."

Someone came forward, reaching for her, and she jerked away from his hand. Mukisa tried to squeeze through to see better, and saw her father pushing his way between the stranger and her mother, struggling to keep him away. The crowd of villagers moved inward, some of them stepping forward to try and pull the intruder back. Unable to push her way through, Mukisa settled on watching her mother, who was still partially in view. Her mask was firmly in place, but Mukisa could tell by her shaking hands that she was terrified.

"Adranna," the strange man sneered, leaning toward her as best he could. His back was hunched, his shoulders distorted even past the effects of age, with large bulges protruding from them. "Where are my grandchildren? I know you had two of those bastards. I think it's time you came home and let our family be whole again."

"It was never whole," Marie whispered, fighting to keep her voice steady. "And you're never taking them away from here."

Understanding began to seep into the back of Mukisa's mind. She had heard the stories — stories she nearly had to pry out of her mother in years past, stories about the life she had lived in the Northern Village. *Calam*. Her mother's father.

"You don't belong here," he said, and spat; Marie blinked, letting the saliva dribble down her cheek. "You're coming back with me. To your proper home. It took me sixteen years to find you, but I did. And you've been out of line for too long."

Mukisa had had about enough. No one, of relation or not, was going to spit on her mother and get away with it. She shoved forward, through the crowd, and broke through to her mother. "Mama?" she piped up. "What's going on?"

The look of terror finally broke past the mask, now blatantly displayed across her mother's face. "Honey, get out of here," she breathed.

But Mukisa had already done her damage. Calam's attention shifted to her, and a smirk formed on his lips. "Is this one of 'em?" he sneered, looking her up and down. His eyes sent a shiver down Mukisa's spine — they held red irises, piercing and shrewd.

Forgetting her fear, Marie bolted forward and placed herself between her father and daughter. "Mukisa, please, just go back to work," she hissed, her eyes never leaving Calam.

"Who's he?" Mukisa asked disdain-fully — she knew the answer, but she wasn't about to allow him the satisfaction of her recognition.

"I'm your grandfather."

Mukisa gave him a defiant look. "My mother was mud-born."

Calam's face contorted with rage. "Yes, she was mud-born — and I took her in as my own. I *chose* her. That's more than this bitch can say about you." He laughed darkly. "I'm your grandfather, girlie, whether you like it or not. And the same goes for me, too." He took a step nearer, and the villagers nearest to him, ever the silent mediators, rushed forward to stop him from getting too close. He glared at them. "For cryin' out loud!"

Mukisa stepped out from behind her mother, emboldened by the sudden wall of people between her and this new stranger. "If you're my grandfather," she said, "then that means you're the two-faced, despicable disgrace of a man who dared to touch my mother."

Calam's jaw dropped. He jerked his head and leveled his gaze at Marie. "You been slingin' mud, Adranna? I oughta wash your mouth out with soap for spreadin' that kind of nonsense..." He pushed forward, his strength surpassing those around him, and grabbed Marie roughly by the arm. Beside her, Mukisa gasped, the carcass falling from her shoulder to the ground, and felt her body slipping from the grasp of her own control, her hand moving to her belt and grasping her knife defensively. In a second, the damage was done: deep red blood began to seep from the hole in the side of his shirt, and he staggered forward, loosening his grip on her mother and instead latching onto Mukisa, his hand around her throat, his eyes blazing.

Little pricks of light began to swarm in front of her eyes as her windpipe was forced closed, and she felt her instincts kicking in: the world around her became a blur as she moved — she felt sure that her body was not her own anymore. It now belonged to a fiery demon, full of strength and power and anger, and she was moving, dragging, the shouts of the villagers behind her, cheering her on in their horrified tones. And suddenly she was stooping, pushing, and her vision cleared: her grandfather was below her, and the mud below that, and he was choking, and her hands were performing the act, and then she was pushing him down, ignoring the sharp pains of his kicking feet, ignoring the fire in her head, watching him sink and gurgle and plead with his eyes, those red eyes, and the mud was rising, covering them up and removing those red eyes from her sight, and then hands were on her back and her shoulders and she was being pulled back, screaming and kicking like a child, and there were other screams, and then there was silence.

Mukisa stared idly at the streak of blood

on the grass, saw its trail leading to the field, and then everything went black.

♦

Chancellor expected that to be the end of his and Mukisa's nighttime visits. But the next night, Mukisa came back to the field. And so did Chancellor. In fact, both of them came back for the next several nights, learning to work with each other, even if it was with a begrudging look or an awkward side glance. It wasn't at all a statement that she could put up with his presence, or a silent apology and admittance that he felt her pain… This wasn't about them. This was about Cecilia.

9

The Specters

The first few days of the ban slipped by
quietly. The diggers shifted their focus to
gardening and other odd jobs without much
difficulty at all. The only fuss to be made was
that of Wyatt, who refused to go home. He
joined the gardeners as well, much to the
chagrin of Chancellor and John and everyone
else in the Southern Village, who very quickly
realized that the foreigners who had come to
dig were not digging anymore, and had quite
a few words to say about it.

The problem was, there were no actual
rules preventing a foreigner from gardening,
and so they could not forcibly remove him. But

they could give him living hell, especially when he spoke his protests in the village green every night, calling people to counter the ban on the field.

Mukisa had no qualms with Wyatt causing a little ruckus. Sure, his eager efforts were a little irritating, but after all, the only thing it could really do was potentially shorten the ban... though she highly doubted that possibility. And John remained as well, more as a grumbling, chastising force for Wyatt to reckon with, which especially seemed to irk the villagers, but Mukisa secretly hoped that would spur them into action even quicker.

Chancellor remained, as well. Mukisa had varied thoughts on that.

One day, Marie was summoned just after the workday had come to a close. The children from the Guest House came running, and crowded around her with wide eyes, mumbling. "What's the matter?" she asked, concern rising in her throat. But they didn't say anything; they just pointed.

Marie pushed past them and saw for herself: there, perched on the roof of the Guest House, was a specter, its wings lazily dangling over the doorframe. It would have seemed as if the specter had randomly chosen its resting place, were it not for the way its icy blue eyes roamed the vicinity of the area, shrewdly observing the passersby. It looked as if it was guarding something.

And guarding, it was. Marie saw

movement through the window: it was Catherine, sitting on her bed with her knees up to her tear-streaked chin. The poor child was shaking.

"It won't let her come out," a little boy whispered, tugging on Marie's sleeve. "And it won't let anyone near the door. What's it doing there, Sheriff?"

Marie stared at it for a moment, thinking. Strangely enough, she could not recall a single time that one of the specters had ever landed on any of the houses in the village. They usually kept to themselves, isolated from the people but always looming, always giving a constant reminder of their presence. This one, however, was about to set up shop and disrupt the silent agreement that they had seemed to have for so long.

"Catherine?" she called out, and the specter's eyes snapped fiercely toward the sound of her voice.

At Marie's call, Catherine jumped up and ran to the doorway; but before she reached it, the specter's wings flexed, rising slightly — more a warning than a preparation for action — and she stopped dead. "I can't get out!" she cried in a shrill voice.

Marie eyed the specter. It stared right at her, a wary, challenging look on its face, and a slight hiss escaped from its throat.

She sent the children away, promising them that Catherine would join them shortly, and quickly set off to look for her daughter.

The hunters were just returning with the night's dinner.

Mukisa immediately recognized the look of concern on her mother's face. She gestured to Paul, who fell in line with the two women as they returned to the Guest House.

Mukisa toyed with one of her knives, eyeing the specter carefully. The soft sound of crying could now be heard inside the Guest House. "What if I just anger it?"

"Well, I am hoping that you won't miss, and we won't have to worry about any of its emotions."

"Do you really think that will kill it?" Mukisa asked skeptically.

"We know they don't like shovels," a voice said pointedly behind her. "Why not knives, too?" It was John, standing there with a bin of fruit from the garden balanced in his arms. Mukisa craned her neck and realized a small crowd was beginning to form behind them; the children had the uncompromisable ability to spread word of a situation, and had not failed in this case. She wondered briefly whether it was concern or curiosity that was at the forefront of their minds.

Mukisa glared at John. "Thank you for your contribution," she snapped, then turned back to a stern look from her mother. She rolled her eyes. "Okay, fine, I'll give it a try. But at least have people stand back… I'm afraid it's gonna lash out."

Marie nodded and motioned for the

crowd to move back. She then called out, soliciting another hiss from the specter: "Stand away from the windows, Catherine!" They heard a faint rustling from inside, then silence.

Mukisa sized up the specter, took aim, and sent her knife swiftly through the air. It hurtled past, barely grazing the specter as it picked itself up and swooped down from the roof, shrieking. The crowd behind her murmured in agitation, and Mukisa stumbled backwards, letting out a yell as the specter swept right through the area in which she had just been standing…

And promptly rode the wind back up to its position on the roof.

Mukisa stood, dusting herself off, and glared at the creature, motivation surging through her veins. What was it doing? she wondered. It could go after any child in the village, if it had torment on its mind. Why choose this one?

The specter shifted its weight, its talons gripping the doorframe firmly, and tilted its head like it was listening. It let out a soft, inquisitive cry.

Paul stepped forward and handed Mukisa another knife, and upon a quick moment's thought, she grabbed a second knife from her collection, holding one in each hand.

"Wait," Marie said hesitantly, looking back and forth between knives and talons.

"And what?" Mukisa asked. "Wait for the

specter to get bored and go in there with her? Yeah, okay." She gave her mother an admonishing look. Turning back to the specter, she gave it her full attention, and lobbed one of the knives straight at it. This time when it took flight and came around at her, shaking the ground with its scream, Mukisa was prepared: she held up the other knife and wielded it, swiping at the specter. It caught on its back leg, drawing cold, blue blood.

The specter made its circle again, then suddenly came straight back at Mukisa, talons reaching. She swung at it with the knife, but the specter was quick, maneuvering and wrenching the knife from her hands before shooting up into the sky.

Mukisa fell back onto the ground and stared at the receding specter, her knife clutched in its claws. She stood up shakily. The door to the Guest House opened, and Catherine bolted out and straight into Marie's arms, sobbing.

"What the hell just happened?" Paul asked, still staring up at the specter in disbelief.

Mukisa glanced over at him, trying to catch her breath. But before she could respond, the knife plummeted from the sky and plunged straight down into the soil below her, just inches from her body. She jumped back, eyes wide, and Catherine gave a little shriek, skittering away as Paul and Marie rushed toward Mukisa.

"Are you okay?" Paul asked as she grabbed onto his arm, trying to steady herself.

"Yeah, I'm fine," she said, taking deep breaths. Her eyes narrowed, and a vindictive smile crossed her face as she looked up at what was now just a dot overhead. "At least we know they bleed."

♦

The night found Chancellor and Mukisa side by side in the mud once more, diligently digging. Their words to each other were few, more from a lack of topic than from spite, a fact which both of them (though Mukisa would never admit it) were grateful for. Occasionally one would let out a little gasp, and the other would turn expectantly, but it was always a false alarm. And they would resume their digging, as if neither of them knew the other existed.

But Chancellor's mind was constantly churning, trying to produce a topic that would instigate conversation. Here was his daughter — his own blood — and he couldn't manage to hold a steady conversation with her. She seemed all the more inclined tonight to pretend that she was mute.

After a hearty bout of silence, he made a feeble effort. "Your mother said Cecilia was going to be a digger."

Mukisa tensed when he spoke, their silent agreement now broken; at first she did not respond, instead continuing to dig, her head down. But after a moment, she said, "She *was* a digger. Is. If the roles were reversed, if I was under the field and she was the one digging, she would have found me by now. Me, and three other people, she was that good."

Chancellor gave a small smile.

"And now…" She sighed. "There's not a chance in the world we'll find her, just the two of us. At least before we had a fifth of the village on this field, looking. Now, the odds are pretty low."

"Don't get me started," Chancellor muttered. "I'm not too thrilled about the ban either."

Mukisa looked up, surprised. "Really?"

Chancellor gave her an admonishing look. "Would I be digging now if I wanted people to stay off the field? The whole reason I'm here is to see Cecilia rescued, Mukisa. Being pleased with a ban would be counter-intuitive. No… the ban was not one of your mother's finest decisions, if you ask me."

Mukisa smiled slowly. "Yeah, she can make some pretty stupid decisions sometimes."

Chancellor raised an eyebrow, and looked up to see her watching for a reaction. He shook his head. "I'm going to refrain from any comment," he said. "I have a sneaking suspicion that anything I say against her will find its way back to her ears."

"It's not like it matters, you aren't together anymore, anyway."

He could still feel her watching him, but concentrated on the mud in front of him. "That doesn't mean that I want a hostile relationship with her."

He still felt her eyes on him, and sighed. He knew where this was going. He glanced up and locked eyes with her. "Mukisa. Just because I'm back in town doesn't mean your mother and I are going to get back together."

Mukisa looked startled. "That's not what I meant—"

"Well… in case it was. It's not going to happen."

"Okay." She stared at him, puzzled. "I'm not hoping it will. I mean—" She sighed.

Chancellor chuckled. "Your mother and I have our separate worlds now. There is a part of me that will always love her… but it's more of an… 'I love remembering the times that we had' kind of love."

Mukisa snorted. " 'I love who you used to be, but not who you are now'." Chancellor gave her a look, and she laughed. "No, I understand, I do."

"I hope so. Because it's important for you to know… if we don't get back together, it doesn't mean that I don't love *you*."

Mukisa rolled her eyes. "I'm nineteen. That's a conversation you should save for Cecilia."

"All right, all right." They continued digging, and Chancellor smiled. Despite Mukisa's dismissal, he had a sneaking suspicion he really had just assuaged her fears.

Suddenly, a noise from the darkness reached their ears. Mukisa and Chancellor spun around, only to see a gangly shadow stooping awkwardly in the moonlight.

Chancellor squinted. "Wyatt, is that you?"

"Um, yes," came the response. "Sorry, I didn't realize there were people out here…"

Mukisa rolled her eyes. "What are you doing up?"

"I just, um, couldn't sleep, and I—" Wyatt hesitated. "Wait. Sheriff, is that you? And… Mukisa, is it?"

He took a few eager steps closer, joining them on the field. "Well, damn it all, if you didn't have the same intentions I had!"

Chancellor glanced cautiously over at a brooding Mukisa. "Did you come to dig, Wyatt?"

"Well, yeah, of course," Wyatt said, plopping down beside them. "I've been going on and on about getting out on this field, and I finally realized I should probably just do it, you know? I mean, yeah, the ban is almost over, but still. Every day that goes by is another chance for that specter to do some serious damage… we might as well make it so there are less victims for it to inflict it upon."

Mukisa's frown slowly softened, and she shrugged, returning her focus back to the field. Chancellor glanced back over at Wyatt, who grinned toothily, and the three of them began to dig.

◆

The village was awoken especially early the next morning to the sound of rustling wings. Stepping outside, Mukisa felt her heart fall into her stomach as she counted specter after specter riding the breeze in the air above. Every day the number seemed to grow larger, as if the beasts were gathering their friends from the other villages and forming some kind of army. The idea of their numbers multiplying chilled her to the bone.

But it also infuriated her. It was a necessary fury, one that blossomed under healthy doses of fear; but she was alone in this retaliation. The villagers around them bustled about quietly, their bodies bent on ignoring the specters but their eyes exposing their concern by flitting periodically up to the sky. This quiet repression was nearly more than Mukisa could take. Their fear set out to control them, and they reacted by hiding their emotions; well, Mukisa would react by wearing them on her sleeve. How dare these beasts encroach on their lives, especially today, of all days.

Today was the day that the ban on the field was to be lifted.

Mukisa watched as the diggers went about their morning routines. Wyatt was the only one who looked even remotely excited about the day — the others were getting ready much more sluggishly than the average day. Mukisa sighed. They were waiting for her mother's call. No one would admit that they wanted the ban to remain, but it was clear that no one actually wanted to go out on that field, not when so many specters were watching. Not after what had happened to Martin.

It pained her that the only decision her mother could make that would protect the village was the decision that would prevent Cecilia from being found.

She watched Marie open the door of the Guest House, a group of giggling children pushing past her as she stepped outside. The woman stiffened as she looked at the sky, and after a long moment, turned to look at her daughter, an apologetic look on her face.

Mukisa saw the resolve in her mother's eyes and despaired. She rushed forward, pleading with her whole body. "No, Mama, please—"

"We can't risk it." Marie's voice was shaky; she was still trying to get over the implications of her own decision.

"But Mama—"

"You aren't going to change my mind," she said stoically, though Mukisa noticed that the calm she projected didn't change the fact that she couldn't make eye contact. Mukisa willed her to break, to change her mind, but instead, she smoothed the folds of her dress and began to walk away, toward the field. Mukisa tailed her, roughly grabbing her arm.

"Mama. *You're not even giving her a chance.*"

Her mother gave her a stern look, her eyes flashing. "Mukisa. I am the sheriff of this village. I have a duty to protect everyone, not just my own kin."

Her mask was already up, unwavering and impenetrable. Too bad I already know what's behind it, Mukisa thought. "But you have *more* of a duty to protect your own," she said softly.

Marie abruptly turned and walked away. Mukisa blinked, rage flooding her vision. She *knew* that her mother's heart was thudding against her chest just as much as hers was; she *knew* that behind that mask, behind those strong words, her mother was hoping that she really was making the right decision — sacrificing her own for the good of others, because she felt she had already been enough of a burden on her village.

Mukisa watched the scene unfold like a nightmare. The diggers greeted Marie with silence as she reached the edge of the field; all stared at her, waiting for her word. She looked around at all of them sadly, then stated simply, "Not today."

She saw Wyatt's jaw drop. She watched her father running after her mother as she left the diggers, heard them spitting hushed words at each other. And in all that was said, in all the anger that was exchanged between two ex-lovers fighting over their child, one thing rang in Mukisa's ears.

"Take a look at the sky, Chancellor. The

field is a jealous Mother, and she comes with reinforcements! Anyone who goes out there today is going to be a target for the specters."

Mukisa understood. She saw that whatever was making the specters more plentiful was causing a safety hazard. And she understood that as much as it pained her, lifting the ban was simply unacceptable.

But this did not prevent her from returning to the field that night after everyone had gone to sleep, and her father and Wyatt were not thwarted either. The three of them picked up their silent game, none of them surprised about each other's presence.

They worked diligently, occasionally letting out a grunt of hope, their efforts becoming immediately frustrated as whatever they had felt under the mud slipped out of their clutch. At this point, it was unclear whether they were actually grasping at people under the mud, or whether their exhausted minds were just playing tricks on them.

But tonight produced a different result: this time, Mukisa's gasp was coupled with, "Daddy!", her eyes wide and hopeful, both arms submerged in the mud. Chancellor quickly scooted in to help her, and Wyatt, who had wandered several yards away, stood, making his way over to help. Father and daughter began to pull the limp body of a girl up through the soil.

As they struggled against the suck of the mud, it became more and more visible that the girl they were rescuing was maybe ten or eleven years old. Mukisa scooped mud away from the girl's neck, revealing a long mess of matted hair, and suddenly let go of the girl, her face downcast. Swearing, Chancellor quickly tried to catch the weight of the girl as she began to slip back down into the mud. He glanced sharply at Mukisa. "What are you doing?!"

Mukisa did not reply. She brought trembling hands to her face, closing her eyes and shutting out the world around her. She heard him crying out, heard Wyatt rushing over to help, and the struggle of the mud, and knew that they had lost the girl. Her eyes flickered open, and she watched the end of their desperate search.

It took them a few moments to give up entirely. Chancellor sighed, wiped the sweat from his brow, and stared at his daughter, her lifeless eyes staring right back at him. "Why did you let her go?" he asked in disbelief.

Mukisa's thoughts seemed to jolt back into focus. She looked down at the mud, bewildered. "I... I didn't mean to..."

"You can't just pick and choose who you rescue from the field, Mukisa!" Chancellor barked. "It doesn't work like that! You can't just push everyone who's not Cecilia back under the mud!"

Mukisa stared at him, shocked. "That's not what I was trying to do!" she cried. "How dare you even say that—"

She got to her feet shakily, nearly tipping

over, and Chancellor reached out to steady her. "Mukisa, when was the last time you got any sleep?"

Mukisa blinked, the question taking her by surprise. She could not remember... certainly before she had started digging at night.

"Let go of me," she hissed, shoving his arm away.

"Go to bed, Mukisa." He grabbed her by the shoulders and strong-armed her off of the field, despite the punches and kicks she laid on him. Wyatt stared at the scuffle nervously, unsure of how to interfere. Father and daughter both had a stubborn streak.

"Stop it!"

"*Go to bed.*"

He roughly let her go, his body blocking her from returning to the field, and she fumed at him for a moment, then stormed off toward her house, roughly pushing past Wyatt. They watched her hesitate at the door, looking over at the Guest House and listening for sounds, then turn back and give her father a glare before slipping inside.

Only after she had disappeared did he allow himself a smile at the fact that she had called him "Daddy".

10

The Announcement

Mukisa sat, leaning up against the dried mud wall of her house, diligently sharpening her knives in preparation of the day's hunt. As with Paul, the act was soothing to her, but perhaps her reasons were a little different, for at the moment she was battling an array of emotions. Last night's slip up was today's guilt trip, and she couldn't get the mistake out of her mind.

A little girl had nearly been unearthed. She would have been cleaned up and sleeping off the exhaustion of the field in the Guest House right now. But instead, Mukisa had let her go. Her father's accusation echoed through her head, and she shuddered. She refused to let herself believe that she had let go because of who the girl *wasn't*... but the thought kept creeping back into her mind.

That brought the tally up to two people who were lost to the field because of her. Her thoughts strayed to the face of her grandfather, sinking below the mud, red eyes bugging, and the blade she was sharpening slipped, nicking her finger. She stuffed her finger into her mouth before the dripping blood would trigger the memory of the blood leaking from Calam's wound.

She suspected she would always have the horror of what she had done dancing around in the shadows of her mind, no matter how hard she tried to push it out. But now it had danced its way to the foreground. And it wasn't just what she had done; it was the implications of what she had done that haunted her. There was something that Mukisa had never been able to say aloud, something which made this memory even more frightening, and made the knife sharpening even more soothing: everyone just assumed that Mukisa felt remorse. And in a way she did — she felt awful for the way she had reacted against a human being — but not against that particular human being. That man had had it coming to him. When it came to protecting her family, Mukisa was not about to play nice with an abusive, terrible man... a man that made her mother hide herself from the world, and blame herself for things she had nothing to do with.

So when everyone assumed that Mukisa felt bad about pushing her grandfather into the mud, they were wrong. She had done the right thing. Perhaps it hadn't been the best timing, or the best way to go about it, but she felt no shame in protecting her family.

Or at least that's what she kept telling herself. An inkling of doubt was beginning to crowd into her mind. Was pushing someone under the mud, even someone who deserved it, really the right thing? Perhaps it was just the thing that had felt good at the time.

And she still wasn't giving herself the greatest track record out on that field. How was she supposed to save her sister if the only experience she had with the field was pushing people under, not pulling them out? Never let anyone be within arm's length when you're near that field, she thought.

Except for her father. Apparently she didn't care enough about his safety to include him in "anyone".

Except she did. She had called him Daddy. She hadn't called him that in years. Never mind that her body had been wracked with fatigue, or that she felt these days that her mouth was in charge of her mind and not the other way around... *she had called him Daddy*.

She looked up, her finger still in her mouth, and saw Mama Nina standing over her. The old woman smiled, her eyebrows raised in a question. Mukisa furrowed her brow defensively. "My knife slipped."

Mama Nina began the slow descent into a seated position beside her. When she had finally situated herself, she remained silent. Mukisa gave her a sidelong glance. "Is there something you wanted?"

"I was going to ask you the same question," Mama said amiably. When Mukisa continued to stare, she prodded her gently with her elbow. "You looked like you needed a talk."

"I'm fine," Mukisa said, unconvincingly. Mama just smiled and stared out at the rest of the village, taking in the morning bustle. Mukisa sighed. "I was just thinking about my father," she said slowly.

"Wondering why he left you?"

Mukisa was startled at the bluntness of her words. She gave the old woman a challenging look. "Why couldn't I be wondering why he came back?"

"In order to wonder why he came back, you must first wonder why he left."

Mukisa gave a small huff. "Are you sure I looked like I needed a talk?"

"I'm positive," Mama said, a twinkle in her eye.

Mukisa gave her a begrudging look. "Well, the leaving part isn't too difficult to figure out. He didn't want to have to deal with a murderer for a daughter. No one ever told him when I was born that I would turn into *this*, that he would have to put in a little extra love — and when he didn't have it, he left."

Mama stared at her for a moment, her thoughts unintelligible. Finally, she spoke. "Some people have a very narrow perception of how the world works. They build their world around them, to their exact specifications, and when something crashes into that world and knocks it over, they will pick up the broken pieces and, instead of keeping them for the potential they still have, they will throw them out." She smiled. "But those broken pieces can sometimes build the tallest tower, when given the chance."

"I'm not broken," Mukisa said heatedly.

"On the contrary. You are a tall tower." Mama hesitated, then sighed. "Your father saw you in a different light. He saw that his baby had become someone that he was not comfortable with. And so he rejected this new person — whether he knew he was doing it or not — and kept his old perception of you with him as he went."

"Why are you trying to excuse him?"

"I am doing nothing of the sort. I will not excuse or forgive his actions — I believe he did the worst thing he could do in running from his family. I simply aim to reveal the inner workings of his mind. He is human. Let there be no misconstruing what that means."

Mukisa rolled her eyes. "Why do I have to know the inner workings of his mind? If he's a horrible person regardless of his reasoning, why can't I just continue to hate him the way

I've been hating him?"

"I never said he was a horrible person," Mama Nina said in alarm. "Just that he made a horrible decision. Please know the difference. Goodness, Mukisa, are you a horrible person because of a decision you made five years ago?"

Mukisa stared at her, afraid to answer. It wasn't five years ago that she was worried about anymore. She quickly changed topics. "Mama... You said before that you had a theory."

Mama Nina hesitated. Perhaps she was adjusting to the change of conversation; or perhaps she wasn't happy with the change. "I suppose I did say that," she replied, frowning.

"It was about why the specter is under the mud." Mukisa squinted at her. "Do you know something that you're keeping a secret?"

"Oh, that was just thoughts from an old lady," Mama said quickly. "I... I only meant..." She frowned. "You see, we don't know that much about the specters. For instance, we know that we come from the field. It is our womb."

Mukisa nodded. "Most of us."

Mama nodded back, giving a wink. "Most of us. And... well, we've never seen the specters as infants... And I've never seen a pregnant specter. Now, it could be that the ones with child are kept protected, and their young are concealed safely in the forest — though I've never heard of the hunters stumbling upon a den of specters. In fact, we haven't seen for sure whether they have eggs or carry their babies the way your mother carried you, or if specters are even capable of having children. We have never bothered to study the specter."

Mukisa raised an eyebrow. "And with good reason; they attack us whenever they come close enough to study."

Mama Nina smiled thoughtfully. "The point is, there is very little we know about the specters. So to find one under the mud... who is to say that isn't a normal occurrence?"

Mukisa stared at her, unsettled. "You mean that they're also somehow birthed in the belly of the field?" She thought for a moment, then shook her head. "But we never see them surfacing."

Mama hesitated. "Like I said, there is very little we really know."

There was something about the look on Mama's face that unnerved Mukisa even more. She frowned. "I thought that hearing this theory would ease my fears, but I think it's done the opposite."

Mama Nina pursed her lips, then patted Mukisa's hand. "Don't worry about it. It wasn't a very good theory, anyway." She eased herself up from the ground. "I'll let you go back to your knives. The last thing I want is to prevent you from having the best hunting conditions..." She hesitated, then gave a sad smile. "I shouldn't be so eager to interrupt the ways that we keep this village intact."

Mukisa watched her amble away, and sighed, feeling a knot of uncertainty settle into her gut. Lately, her conversations with Mama Nina were more upsetting than soothing.

♦

Mukisa awoke hazily to muffled whispers; she opened her eyes to see bright sunlight peeking through the trees above her, a circle of heads peering down at her. She quickly tried to sit up, and felt hands pushing her back down to the ground. Several people surrounded her, though they were too blurry to make out who they were.

"Don't get up." She focused her eyes on the person closest to her: it was Anthony, the man's crinkled eyes expressing worry. "You had quite the fall."

The memory of it flooded back into her mind: perching in a tree, aiming at the unsuspecting doe, feeling her foot slip, and… and then she must have fallen. Damn tree.

"I don't remember…" She reached up and touched her head cautiously. To her surprise, her hands immediately felt for the bead, which still rested upon her forehead. "I didn't land on my head or anything, did I?"

The old hunter shrugged. "We just heard the noise and came running."

"Where's Paul?"

Anthony smiled softly. "We just sent Harper to look for him. He'll meet you back in the village."

"I'm sure I'm fine—" Mukisa started to sit up again, but a dull throbbing echoed in the back of her head. She cringed. "I just have a small boulder embedded in my skull."

Anthony chuckled. He and another hunter reached forward and lifted her up, draping her arms around their shoulders. "Well, until that boulder has worked its way out, I think you need a bed."

♦

Marie knew it would be Paul before she even answered the door. And there he was, clearly restraining himself from just barging into the house. She quickly reassured him with a smile. "She's fine."

He gave up all pretense of decorum and pushed past her. Mukisa lay in bed, hands fidgeting over her blankets as she talked to Mama Nina. Paul approached the two of them, offering a relieved smile. "I heard you fell out of your tree?"

"I thought it was time I found a new one," Mukisa said lightly, reaching out and taking his hand. "Took you long enough. Were you on the east side?"

Paul nodded. "I had already reached the mountains by the time Harper found me. You couldn't have injured yourself earlier in the workday?"

Mukisa gave him a small shove, rolling

her eyes. Mama Nina stood up, offering Paul her chair. "She's on sick watch," she said. "We don't know what that fall did to her head."

"No sleep until tomorrow," Mukisa said. "Doctor's orders."

"Well, that won't be too much of a change," Paul said offhandedly. Marie glanced over sharply, and caught sight of Mukisa cutting him a look. He quickly added, "Because none of us have been getting sleep with all that's been going on."

Marie frowned. "I thought we'd take shifts keeping her awake," she said. "Would you like to start?"

Paul looked at the floor for a moment, then shook his head. "I'll take the later shift."

Mukisa raised her brow. "Oh, fine, thanks," she muttered, dropping his hand dramatically.

"What? I'll be back. I just have to… you know… hunt."

"I'll take the first shift," Mama Nina offered. "It's not like this old woman has a job to attend to anyway."

Marie smiled. "Yes, once you get past the medical attention and the teaching and counseling that you provide, you're really quite useless."

"All in a day's work, my dear." She waved her hands at Paul. "Go back to work."

"I'll be back." He kissed Mukisa lightly on the forehead and headed toward the door. Marie watched him go; there was something on his mind, that was for sure, but alas, she couldn't read him as well as her daughter could. Which was fair... she wasn't the one marrying him, after all.

But if she had only read him vaguely, she had still read him correctly: there *was* something on his mind. Paul went straight to the garden, where Chancellor was working. He had made a guess that no one had told Mukisa's father about her fall, and he was right. Chancellor immediately rushed to her house, oblivious to Paul's insistence that she was fine.

He rather rudely barged into the house, startling the three women inside. Marie gave Chancellor a stern look from her place beside Mukisa's bed, and Mama Nina gave him an admonishing glance. "Well, thank the heavens we were all decent," she chided, nonetheless prodding Marie and motioning for her to rise and offer the man her seat. Marie did so a little reluctantly.

Chancellor leaned in towards his daughter, a worried expression splayed across his face. "Why didn't someone tell me that you were hurt?"

"You're asking *me* this?" Mukisa laughed. "I'm the injured one, I don't take the responsibility of running around, letting everyone know the latest news. And besides, it's not like I'm near death. I'm fine. I'm just not allowed to hunt for a few days," she added bitterly.

"You're on sick watch," Chancellor reminded her. "That's not fine."

Mama Nina stepped forward, giving a small smile. "Just a precaution. You remember, we take our falls seriously here, whether they're serious or not."

"And I thank you for that. But you," Chancellor said, turning back to Mukisa, "have to be more careful! You know you wouldn't have had such a fall if you weren't so exhausted." He ignored Mukisa's pointed look and continued. "I knew I shouldn't have let you stay up digging with me. It's dangerous for a child to lose so much sleep—"

It took less than a second for the meaning of his words to sink in. Marie was appalled; Mama Nina looked like she had just remembered a very important task that she had to do and walked promptly to the door, sending Mukisa a sympathetic glance on her way out.

Marie had momentarily forgotten to keep her mask in place; the rage was extremely apparent on her face. "Mukisa, have you been digging?"

"No, Mama!"

"Don't you lie to me, Mukisa."

Mukisa glared at her father. "Well, no one else will go within fifty feet of that damn field, and I'm not about to wait around for you all to come to your senses. And he's doing it too, and Wyatt, I'm not the only one—"

"Chancellor, really, I thought you had more sense than that—"

"I'm the one who made the decision, Mama! I'm nineteen years old, I can make my own decisions. Contrary to what *some* people believe," she said, shooting a vicious glance at Chancellor, "I'm not a child anymore."

"But you are a hunter," he replied. "You need your energy. I realize now I should never have let you on that field."

"Oh, that is such a lie. You *loved* it. You got to play 'Father, Daughter' every night, trying to get close to me."

Chancellor looked hurt by her words. Marie placed her hands on her temples, sighing. "You're not going back on that field, Mukisa."

"Like hell I'm not—"

"End of discussion! I will not lose you, too, I will not!"

Chancellor was not sure he had ever heard Marie's voice reach that pitch before. He stood, gingerly reaching out a hand as Marie tried to control her breathing. She pushed him away and turned toward the wall, regaining her composure. Chancellor and Mukisa exchanged apprehensive looks. When she turned back around, there was a look of determination on her face. "This leaves me no choice, Mukisa. If you're going to act like a child, well, then we'll treat you like a child. You will not only be on sick watch until the morning, but I am issuing a guard watch as well, indefinitely."

Mukisa looked like she had just been stabbed with her own knife. "No! That's not fair!"

"Wait, what does that mean, exactly?"

Chancellor asked in bewilderment.

"We will assign people to watch her overnight to ensure that she doesn't go anywhere near the field. Maybe I should put a watch on you as well?"

Chancellor locked eyes with her. "Marie, there is nothing that will keep me away from those fields, even one of your stupid bans. I won't go against your wishes in public and undermine your authority, and I will certainly back you in your wishes to keep Mukisa off the field, but I *will* go out on that field every night, and dig until I find my daughter."

"And I hold the same stance!" Mukisa cried. "I'm digging whether you like it or not—"

"Difference between you and me, Mukisa," Chancellor cut in, "is that I won't have my father standing between me and the field, and you will. If I have to spend the whole night keeping you off, then I'll do that, too. But know that you'll be preventing me from getting any digging done."

Mukisa looked like a wolf being cornered by two hunters. Behind her snarl, they could see her mind rampaging with thoughts. "You can't do this! You can't keep me off of that field!"

"Honey, I'm getting a little tired of arguing about this," Marie said plainly. "We *can*, and we *will*."

She fumed at the two of them. "Oh, of course, *now* you would, after all your differences, find common ground in restricting your daughter," she spat. "Then what am I supposed to do? I can't hunt; people are going to be watching me sleep… you might as well just throw me in a cell and push food under the door!"

"Stop being so dramatic, Mukisa. For once, act your age."

Marie watched the inner workings of her daughter's mind present itself on her face as something suddenly seemed to snap. She began to smile, a smile that made Marie extremely concerned about what the next words that would come out of her mouth would be. "Fine. I'll go along with your little watch. But let me remind you, there is one way that you can't prevent me from doing anything. It is every bride's prerogative to cross that field and meet her groom in the middle on the day of her wedding. That is a tradition you can't break!"

Marie felt the blood drain from her face. "Don't be ridiculous. You haven't even set a date yet."

"Oh, I have now. We're going to be married at the end of this week."

♦

Marie stooped at the foot of the small gray slate, hitching up her dress in her hands and brushing some of the dirt away from the etched letters. They stated simply, "L.C."

She had never seen Mukisa act so childish in her entire life. It wouldn't matter to her if a thousand people had been lost to the field that week... she would have just as soon announced the wedding, and with that same raving smile on her face. It was madness.

A breeze picked up and cooled Marie's face, and she closed her eyes, trying to let her worry fall through the cracks of her mind. It didn't work; it never did. After Mukisa had made her decision, Marie had stayed behind to argue with her, until Mama Nina returned and shooed her out of the house. There was no good in arguing until both their heads had cooled, she had said. But Marie's head was still boiling.

She sighed and opened her eyes, staring at the headstone. You would have been able to handle this, she thought, inhaling deeply and holding the breath inside of her in an attempt to stay afloat in her thoughts. You handled everything. You were the sheriff that I tried to be, the sheriff that the village still wants me to be. You took me in, and fixed my problems, and then I went and mussed them up as soon as you were gone, and now I've got more of them and I'm still alone.

She glanced behind her, at the shaded pathway that led back to the village. This little cemetery was just barely tucked into the woods for safety purposes — it was close enough to civilization that animals wouldn't snoop around and try to dig up the bodies, but far enough that you could have peace when visiting the dead. No one ever did visit, it seemed, except for Marie. No one else had the regrets she had, apparently.

She placed her hand softly on the top of the slate and got to her feet, smoothing out her dress. Coming here would not solve her problems. It would not make Mukisa change her mind. What had led her daughter to make these decisions was good and done, and she could not do anything about it, even if she wished she could. That was the problem with regret: you could only see it as it was happening. Never in time to prevent it.

♦

Paul came for his shift just after sundown. Since the watch had now changed purposes, Mukisa was not pleased with his arrival; she refused to give him the satisfaction of eye contact as he sat himself down beside her bed, holding his spear. "Thought I'd sharpen it while we talked."

"Think that'll keep me in my place?" Mukisa challenged moodily.

Paul sighed. "No, Mukisa, I just need to do it sometime before I set out to hunt tomorrow." There was an awkward silence, in which he produced a whetstone from his pocket and began scraping at the tip of the spear with it. "Why did you announce our wedding?" he asked quietly.

Mukisa buried her face in her hands. "I just want to get it over with."

Paul looked up from his work. "Well, that's encouraging."

"That's not what I meant."

"Then what did you mean? Because I thought this was supposed to be a decision we made together."

Mukisa stared at a frayed stitch on her blanket. "You weren't here when she issued the watch. You don't know what it was like... I felt restricted. I didn't know what else to do, Paul."

"Just so you're aware," Paul said slowly, taking effort with each word, "Our wedding is not a means to rebel against your mother's wishes. I would appreciate it if you didn't treat it that way."

Mukisa stared at him. "You think that's why I announced the wedding? Because I wanted to make my mother mad?"

"Kis, you're very good at getting what you want. It's who you are; it's a part of why I'm marrying you. But the ways that you get what you want are not always attractive. Like lashing out at people."

"Paul, I don't want to marry you to lash out at my mother."

"You know I don't believe you do. But you picked a hell of a time to decide to go through with the wedding, Mukisa."

"I know..."

Paul dropped his spear onto his lap, frustrated. "Do you? Because there are specters swarming around that field, more and more every day. And you want to go out into the middle of it and stand there saying your vows?"

Mukisa shook her head. "They're not going to attack us. And if they do… we're both hunters. We can fight if needed."

"That will be memorable, for our wedding day."

"Besides, I think I've threatened enough of them that they're scared of me, anyway. They definitely won't attack."

"Mukisa, you're flesh-born. Just because you're older doesn't mean they want you any less."

"I can take care of myself, Paul."

Paul nodded, then let out a deep breath, moving onto his next tactic. "And speaking of flesh-borns…" Mukisa knew exactly what he was going to say, and she quickly averted her eyes from his, steeling herself. "I thought you wanted to wait until Cecilia resurfaced."

Silence filled the room for a long moment as Mukisa chewed her lip, struggling for words. Finally she managed quietly, "I've said it before… if we wait for that to happen, we might never get married."

"But that's not what you've thought, going out on the field every night. If we get married, and then Cecilia is found the week after that, you're going to regret jumping into this. And I say this with all the love in my heart, because I do want to get married, I do, but there's always going to be that regret—"

"I *live* in regret, Paul! What do you think the last five years of my life have been like?" She glared at him. "And if you really want to get married, you could put in a little effort yourself. Not once have you offered to help dig. What do you think that says about your role as a betrothed? Not even willing to take risks for the sister of your future wife—"

"That is *not* fair, Mukisa. You never asked me to dig."

"Do I have to?"

Paul shot Mukisa's leveled gaze right back at her. "Well, you've clearly decided that announcing a wedding date without asking me is okay, so maybe I'm a little unclear on the rules in this situation."

"Are you afraid, Paul?"

It wasn't said accusingly, but in surprise. Mukisa had never given any thought to Paul's perception of the field. He had never seemed scared of it, and she had never pressed the matter. But then, everyone had a kind of deep-seated obsession with the field… it was a mix of fear and seduction. No matter how hard you tried, your thoughts always returned to the field. Why would it be any different for Paul?

He looked away. "Just because I'm mud-born doesn't mean I don't have any risk out there, Mukisa. It's not just you that you're dragging into this mess, you know."

"Of course I know that." She hesitated. She knew that now, anyway. "But I'm not ready to let that field dictate how we live our lives. Paul, we risk getting hurt every day when we go out into the forest to hunt. We are predators of predators... we risk attack, and yet we continue to hunt, to put meat on our plates."

"It's different for you," Paul muttered. "You've never been under the field before. To you, the field is just something that swallowed your sister. To you, going onto that field will just be a symbolic gesture in a ceremony. It's not just symbolic for me... I'd be going back to my birthplace."

Mukisa smiled. "But that's the beauty of the symbolic gesture... that it's *just* a little bit more than symbolic."

Paul shook his head. "Let's not avoid the real conversation, Mukisa. I don't want to talk about symbols. I want to talk about why you announced our wedding day."

Mukisa was silent for a moment. She shook her head. "I'm sorry. It's just, these past few weeks... my sister gone... now I can't even hunt..."

"That's just a few days, Kis."

"But it's long enough that I'll go stir crazy."

"So we're getting married so that you'll have something to do?"

Mukisa glared at him. "We're getting married because you're the only good thing I have going for me, Paul. In a time when everything's falling apart, when bit by bit I'm losing everything I have, I want to hold onto the one thing I know will never leave. Please don't leave."

Paul looked surprised. "I'm not going to leave you." He gently took Mukisa's hand. "Kis, I promise you, I'm not going to leave you. And I promise I will help you get Cecilia back. Okay?"

Mukisa nodded. She knew his words were sincere — they were not just words to get her to delay their wedding. Which was a good thing… she looked up at the slow smile on Paul's face, and realized he didn't understand. Just because she had accepted his help didn't mean anything had changed. Her mind was made up. "We're still getting married at the end of the week."

Paul's face dropped to an expression of confusion. He studied her for a moment. Mukisa blinked to keep the tears at bay, and squeezed his hand. He sighed, and squeezed back. "Okay. Okay, we'll get married at the end of this week."

♦

The sound of the door slamming shut awoke Wyatt abruptly, and he propped himself up in his place on the floor, heart beating wildly. It was not yet morning, and he sighed at the soft pattering of rain on the thatched roof. The sound made him faintly glad that he had stopped helping Chancellor dig after Mukisa had ratted them out — Chancellor would not be stopped, but Wyatt was, admittedly, not as brave enough to take on the wrath of the villagers. In hindsight, it had saved him the trouble of digging in waterlogged mud.

He rolled over, sighing, set on getting back to sleep, but the sound of laughter and splashing roused him just moments later. The noise came from outside, and he sleepily stumbled to his feet, opening the door to look out.

He was overwhelmed by the sight before him. Basins covered the ground, spread out across both the green and the square and catching the rain as it fell. He stepped out of the hut, immediately shivering as the droplets began landing on his skin. But the villagers did not seem to care about the cold at all; the entire village was outside, frolicking to and fro amongst the basins, all grinning from ear to ear. Wyatt turned just in time to see Mukisa barreling into him from the side, laughing. "Look at them, Wyatt! They're filling right up!"

She released him from her engulfing embrace, and Wyatt collected himself, grinning. Even whatever animosity she had towards him was forgotten in the bliss brought on by the rain, and so had any pain she may still have from her recent head injury. Beside her but a little more off to the side than normal, Paul stood, and Wyatt caught an air of resistance in his stance, though he smiled all the same.

"You see, Paul?" Mukisa was saying. "It's a sign! The skies want us to get married!"

Wyatt glanced around at the villagers, absorbing their glee. It was the first time he had seen everyone so happy, shrugging off their cares and enjoying… well, enjoying a thing that most people considered unenjoyable. Then again, most people didn't have to walk several miles to have water in their village. Wyatt's spirits were immediately lifted as he watched children giggling in their game of tag, their feet nimbly dodging the scattered basins. It was the middle of the night, and the children had no other dream but to have fun. He quickly joined their game.

Standing off to the side of the hubbub, Chancellor closed his eyes and let the water soak into his clothes, his skin. He had forgotten the joy that rain could bring. It made him glad to be in the Southern Village; and yet, it also brought about a twinge of homesickness. How long would he have to stay here until Cecilia surfaced? The thought rudely popped into his head without his permission.

He opened his eyes, and his gaze almost immediately fell upon Mukisa, laughing and spinning in the rain several yards away. She looked so happy… how many happy moments had he missed while he was in the Western Village?

Feeling a presence beside him, he turned:

Mama Nina stood quietly beside him, watching the villagers as their antics began to wind down.

He nodded in her direction. "I wondered when you might try to talk to me."

She glanced up at him, surprised. "Talk to you? I have talked to you several times since you've arrived, Chancellor."

"I meant, have a chat with me. Like you do. Your famous talks."

Mama chuckled. "I don't know if I would go so far as famous." She sobered, staring out at the village. "Do you intend to stay, Chancellor?"

"I've already said I will stay until we find Cecilia."

"And then you intend to leave."

Chancellor hesitated. "I suppose, yes."

"Why did you come back?"

Chancellor gave her a furious look. "I just explained that. I'm here to find Cecilia."

"We have many talented diggers here, Chancellor. We could notify you of your daughter's return from the mud." Mama was trying to read his face, though he was sure all it displayed at the moment was annoyance.

"I understand that, but I had to be here," he muttered.

"I am not asking you this to rile you up," Mama said, "I am simply asking so that you ask yourself the same question. Why did you come back?"

Chancellor thought for a moment, his

eyes drifting back to his daughter as she twirled around, eyes closed and arms outstretched. "I don't know exactly. I could hardly tell you why I left in the first place."

"Because of your father."

"Yes. He was sick — he was *dying* — I had to see him. But it was more than just that, I think. Otherwise… otherwise I would've come back, right?" He swallowed uncomfortably, and looked to Mama for a response, but she was silent. He returned his gaze to his daughter, still spinning about, except this time there wasn't that feeling of happiness; only of guilt. "I remember when the only thing I had to worry about with my daughter was when she'd reach puberty. I had a hard enough time dealing with the fact that my little girl would eventually get to the point where her body would stir into action, and set off down the path to change… I was worried, you know, with her already volatile nature, about hitting that particular phase of her life. She already made boys cry during playtime, and I could only imagine what would happen when hormones became involved.

"But that was nothing compared to… Well, you know what happened." He hesitated, shrugged. "I think the Western Village had decided that I had somehow gotten pulled into a shifty situation and that I wasn't sure how to get out… so they offered me the position.

"There was never any intent to hurt my family, I never wanted them to be in any sort of pain... in fact, I think if circumstances had been different, I would have insisted that they move to the Western Village with me. Maybe they could now." He frowned. "But at the time, that would not have gone over well. It's just that... I did have a desire to take charge of things, and the position as Sheriff granted me that opportunity. And it's petty, I know, but, well..." Chancellor looked away from Mukisa. "I saw my daughter differently that day," he said slowly, thoughtfully. "I... I wasn't able to shake that image from my mind." He sighed. "I hate that it's true, but when I saw my daughter, I saw... a murderer. I didn't want to see her in that way. And so I distanced myself. I may not have realized that was why, but the reasoning was there all the same."

Mama studied him closely, then glanced out at the crowd. "I know," she said. "And so does she."

Chancellor's heart plummeted.

"And do you still see her that way?" she asked.

He smiled weakly. "Not as much. There are moments when it all flashes back, but I think I see my daughter for who she really is. My beautiful, wonderful daughter." He lifted his gaze back to Mukisa, his heart twinging at her smile.

Mama nodded. "So you came back to absolve yourself of that feeling. And now, when you leave, you will once again rip apart from your family, and leave them again.

But *you* will feel all right."

Chancellor grimaced. "I won't feel all right. But we have our separate lives now."

Mama raised an eyebrow at him, and he squirmed under her stare. "It is interesting to me," she sighed, "that the reason you will leave is because of a situation that you caused to begin with."

With that, she walked away, leaving Chancellor with even more of an ache in his heart.

11

The Cloth

The next day, after the day's work was done, Marie and Mama Nina led Mukisa to the large storage shed in the corner of the village. Very carefully, the three women dragged a large trunk from its belly. Marie took the key out of the folds of her dress and turned it in the big, rusty padlock; it creaked as it opened, and dust particles fled from their prison and into the sunlight.

"Go ahead," Marie said, prodding Mukisa toward the trunk.

Mukisa stooped down and reached inside, lifting a dirty bundled cloth from the trunk and examining it. She whistled. "We have a disgusting ritual," she muttered, laughing a little.

"Nonsense," Mama Nina said. "It is beautiful."

Mukisa stared at the cloth, a glittering in her eyes. Disgusting or not, this cloth had been used throughout the generations, for each wedding ceremony in the village. Even her mother had adorned herself in this very cloth for her own wedding day. It was a tradition of which Mukisa could not believe she was finally taking part. A slow smile spread across her face. "Where's the basin?"

Her mother led her to the washing basin, filled with water. A block of soap sat next to it. Mukisa dropped the cloth into the basin and set to work lathering the soap.

Marie sat on the grass beside her daughter, and Mama Nina gently squeezed their shoulders. "I'll leave you to your washing," she said with a smile.

Mukisa began to scrub at the fabric, grasping it tightly and working it between her fists until a lather began to appear. She looked up to see her mother watching her, a distant look on her face.

"I remember doing this," Marie said.

Mukisa raised her eyebrows in jest. "Oh yeah? How long did it take you?"

She smiled. "A few hours. I was terrible at washing clothes… and a perfectionist."

"I suppose having two kids changed that considerably."

Marie laughed. "I've definitely had the

practice. But back then, I was a mess. I was nervous, I wasn't sure if I was making the right decision…"

"Well, your situation was a little different."

"Everyone's situation is a little different. Doesn't mean we can't have the same fears. It's the unifying purpose of the cloth… each woman who has married in this village has sat at this very basin and scrubbed this cloth with as much detail as you will tonight. Everyone thinks those thoughts they think no one else is thinking… the doubts, the butterflies. But you can find comfort in the fact that others have gone through the same thing you have. At least emotionally."

"But your situation was *really* different. You were a foreigner, marrying another foreigner in a foreign village."

Marie frowned. "I suppose it was. But it didn't hold the same meaning back then. We were uncomfortable with strangers, yes, but we hadn't all scared ourselves into hostility yet."

"That's true."

"You know, the night before your father and I married, when the village was collecting fireflies, we snuck off and went to the lake and went swimming."

"Mama!" Mukisa laughed. "You skipped out on tradition?"

"We did. And it was a blast. We swam around, completely naked, mind you—"

"*Mama*. I don't want to hear that."

"Oh, you're an adult. You'll be telling similar stories to your children one day."

"I will *not*—"

"And your father decided to scoop me up like a baby from the water and threaten to drop me in. And I was kicking and screaming, telling him if he dropped me, our wedding night was not going to go as planned..." Mukisa grinned at that. "...And at that moment, all I was thinking was, I'm making the right decision. I looked at him, water drops glistening on his face, this big grin, and I thought... I'll be happy with this man. No matter what obstacles come our way, I'll be fine as long as I have him by my side. And then he dropped me into the water."

Mukisa laughed, then turned to look at her mother — to really look at her. She had thought it would be uncomfortable to hear stories about the times when her mother and father were still together, but it was actually nice. Maybe it was just the look on her mother's face as she remembered the moment that was worth it. She could remember the last time her mother had smiled, but not the last time that she was happy.

Mukisa thought back on what her father had said, about his love for Marie being more of an "I love remembering the times that we had" kind of love. It was clearly that way with Marie, too: Mukisa saw the anger seeping through all those layers every time he

217

appeared, but she certainly kept some form of affection for him hidden in her heart. Worry edged its way into Mukisa's mind. "What if I have those feelings with Paul, and then he leaves me too?"

Marie glanced sharply at her, then reached for her and pulled her into an embrace, ignoring the suds that slid down their arms. "All women may share the same emotions, but we do not share the same outcomes. You will not have to go through what I went through. Disaster was drawn towards me long before your father ever came into the picture, and that was what pushed him away. You don't have that same destiny."

"How do you know?"

Marie pulled back and stared into her eyes. "Do you love him?"

Mukisa bit her lip, smiling. "Yeah, I do."

"And he sure as hell loves you. And if you work at it, you can make sure nothing stands in the way of that."

Mukisa smiled, but waited, seeing the look in her mother's eyes... it was a look that said she wasn't quite finished. And she didn't disappoint. "But you don't have to get married right now."

"*Mama...*"

"I'm being serious, Mukisa. The field is incredibly dangerous right now! Just consider—"

"Mama. Would it make you feel better if I brought my knife out on the field with me?"

Marie stared guardedly at her for a moment. "I guess...at least you'd have a way of protecting yourselves against the specters. But—"

"*Mama*. We're going to be fine. I will draw blood from any specter who thinks otherwise."

Marie sighed and kissed Mukisa's forehead. "I know, I can't change your mind. Just... please be careful. You've seen what that mud can do, specters or not."

Mukisa nodded, then thought for a moment. "Mama... do you regret being with Daddy?"

Marie shook her head. "Of course not. I wouldn't have been able to have you if I hadn't met him."

Mukisa gave her an admonishing look. "I'm not asking if you regret having me or Cecilia. I'm asking if you regret your relationship with him."

Marie pulled away and sat back in her spot beside Mukisa, staring at the ground. Caught off guard, she had not had the time to put up her mask, and her uncertainty splayed across her face. Mukisa bit her lip, regretting the question — it would only send her mother into a whirlpool of doubt.

After a brief moment, Marie smiled; but it was a sad smile. She couldn't even bring herself to look Mukisa in the eye as she answered. "Yes. I do."

"Why?"

The question came so impertinently out of Mukisa's mouth that she was startled to hear her own voice speak it. Marie gazed at

Mukisa for a moment before answering. "We were already having problems when he left for the Western Village," she confided. "It wasn't just the situation that kept him away. It was that our relationship had broken its last thread. It had been dangling for some time, and after that, there just wasn't any hope. I think… I think if I had been a little more sensible, I could have made things work. But as it happened, we ended up apart because we weren't right for each other."

"But you were right for each other for so long—"

"No, honey. I just wanted us to be right for each other."

Mukisa stared at her mother in silent disagreement. A thing couldn't be broken unless it was whole before. But the woman cleared her throat, ready to move on. "Let's not dwell on the mistakes that I've made," she said lightly. "This is your night. Your *week*… It's your life, in fact, and it'll be far better than mine ever was. I don't need to worry you with these things."

Mukisa studied her for a moment, a terrible burden settling on her chest. Her smile had lost its happiness again, and Mukisa herself had scared away the rare moment. She sighed and returned to her washing, frowning over the grime that seemed to be ingrained in the fabric. "How many weddings has this cloth been through? I mean, I know it has meaning behind it, but maybe we should just get a new cloth."

Marie chuckled, perhaps relieved to be done with the conversation. "It will come out. But no one said it won't be difficult. It's a process of renewal… whatever dirt and grime you've collected over the years, now is the time to get it all out. You're turning a new leaf tomorrow. And it will take effort."

Mukisa glanced at her wearily. "It doesn't even feel like it will be that much of a change. We'll still be living in the same village, with the same people. Same relationships, same memories. Same past."

"But you can make a personal decision to feel different. Mukisa, I know you've had a less-than-average childhood, and I am to blame for that, but… what people think of you is not who you are. There are so many better ways to describe who you are than what has happened in the past. These things, they… they stain us, but no stain is really permanent. And if you're having trouble getting the stain out, then you're at least trying to get that stain out—do you see what I'm saying?"

Mukisa rolled her eyes. "Yes, Mama."

"Even if you aren't the kind of person that you want to be at the moment, what you *want* to be says something about who you are. With a moment like this, you can clear out the old mess of obstacles that you've come across in your life so far, and make that goal a little easier to reach."

Mukisa wished her mother would take her own words to heart. The woman stood, squeezing her daughter's shoulder, and left her to her work. Mukisa stared at the cloth before her and sighed. It was going to be a long night.

♦

The night before the wedding was to take place, the entire village gathered in the square with their jars, the little ones holding onto them with gleeful faces. The tradition of catching fireflies for the wedding ceremony was a favorite among young and old alike, and it was all the adults could do to keep the children from taking off into the woods to start early.

But the adults were somewhat distracted this time. The specters, who normally disappeared at nightfall, had decided to stay up late with the rest of the village, perching in the trees surrounding the borders and murmuring quietly to each other. About an hour after the sun went down they did begin to dissipate, creeping further into the forest to sleep, but this did not stop the worry that had already etched itself onto the villagers' faces. Even when the last had been gone for a fair amount of time, the fact that any of them had lingered at all made many wonder if they were actually sleeping, or lying in wait.

Marie stood with her arms folded,

staring into the shadowy mess of trees before her. Mama Nina sidled up beside her, and she nodded to her in acknowledgement. "This place is beginning to feel like a prison," she said distantly, clenching her fists and stepping toward the woods.

A single speck of light flitted from inside the forest to the edge of the square, dancing in the twilight. Marie pushed aside her thoughts and put on a smile, turning to face the assembly of villagers. "I see our first firefly is trying to welcome us into its home! Does everyone have their jars?" A murmur of ascent rippled through the crowd. Marie nodded. "Then let's go."

The fireflies did wonders to soothe the tension of the night. The soft orbs of light bobbed like living stars, blinking in and out as they made their silent mating calls. Wyatt watched a line of giggling children run by, jars clutched tightly in their hands, and stared down at his own jar, watching their fun through the reflection of the glass.

A firefly flicked past his nose, and he started. John appeared beside him, smirking. "You're never going to catch them if you let *them* catch *you* off guard!"

Wyatt grinned sheepishly, and swiftly reached out with his jar, cupping his hand over the opening and catching the firefly.

"There you go," John laughed. He stooped and looked at the firefly, hovering inside the glass. "I guess now the next challenge is to catch more than one without the others getting out of the jar." He scratched his head thoughtfully.

"What do we do with them once we've caught them?" Wyatt asked curiously.

"They're going to light the wedding reception tomorrow. Or so I've been told. Pretty cool, huh?"

Wyatt smiled. "Maybe we can take this tradition back to the Western Village!"

John gave him a thin smile. "Good luck with that."

Wyatt felt a tug on the hem of his shirt, and turned to see Catherine staring up at him, clutching her own jar protectively. "Hey, Catherine," he said, picking the little girl up and smiling at her. Just yesterday, she had been adopted by a couple who lived right past the gardens, and the look on her face reflected her contentment. She held her jar close to her, staring at the single glowing light captured within.

"Look, you've got competition," John said, pointing to her jar.

"Have you already caught a firefly, Catherine?" Wyatt gasped. "I'm impressed!"

Catherine giggled, staring at her prize, then suddenly looked serious. "Is it a baby firefly?" she asked.

Wyatt looked closely. "No, I don't think so. I don't think baby fireflies have wings. Were you worried you had separated a baby from its mama?"

She nodded, biting her lip. "Do baby

fireflies glow too?"

Wyatt glanced at John, curious. John raised his eyebrows. "What are you looking at me for?"

Wyatt thought for a moment, then turned back to Catherine. "You know, I have no idea. I don't know if I've ever seen a baby firefly, so I can't be sure."

She sighed longingly. "I want to glow."

John chuckled. "Then you'd better turn into a firefly."

Catherine grinned at him. "Will you help me find a baby firefly?" she asked, holding out her jar. His eyes widened. Wyatt hid a smile; he was pretty sure that once John had grown up, he had made it a point not to talk to children... it just wasn't his niche.

"I don't know if we'll be able to find one..." John gave Wyatt a pleading look, and Wyatt laughed.

"Come on, the three of us should be able to find one," he said. John sent him a sharp look, but his glare softened as Catherine squealed and reached for him, transferring herself into his arms. Wyatt led them, Catherine with an excited grin and John with his eyes wide, further into the forest.

They brushed past Mukisa and Paul as the couple walked slowly through the throngs of villagers, Mukisa pinching the hem of Paul's sleeve absentmindedly. The world around her was a softly glowing dream, but the tension remained in her heart. Just a few yards off, she saw her fellow hunter, Anthony, and his husband, walking hand in hand: a touching moment from an elderly couple.

She smiled. "Paul." He turned towards her, and she raised an eyebrow. "Let's get out of here."

Puzzled, he shook his head. "But the fireflies—"

"So what? Let's go have some time to ourselves."

She watched him work out the dilemma in his head; he finally smiled.

The two of them disappeared into the thick of the forest around them, barely missed as the villagers went about their antics. Mama Nina, however, always with a watchful eye, smiled at their departure. She clasped her hand around Marie's wrist as they walked together. "Tomorrow's approaching fast. How do you feel?"

"I feel… conflicted." Marie shrugged. "My baby's gone and grown up. She's become independent, and in some ways that's a good thing…"

"But in some ways, it is bad?"

Marie stared at Mama. "Maybe. I don't know." She sighed. "They're going to go out on that field tomorrow and fall under, Mama. I just know it."

"Then call it off."

Marie was silent for a moment. "I can't."

"Why not?"

"Because… Mukisa's got her mind made

up, and I'm afraid if I stop her now, I might push her away from me. And I don't doubt her in a match against the specters... but she's never tried to fight the field before."

"You fear that she will have to tomorrow?"

Marie frowned. "Yes. But fear isn't a good enough reason to prevent a wedding from happening. How can I stop them from having the happiest day of their lives just because I *fear* that something will go wrong?" She grimaced. "Maybe I'm just projecting my failed marriage onto her, and the field is an easy excuse."

Mama chuckled, and squeezed her hand tightly. "Whatever happens, it will happen for a reason, my dear. Even you cannot prevent fate."

Marie smirked. "I'm living proof of that fact, I know. I just wish I could ensure that my daughter's fate is a happy one."

Mama smiled. "Perhaps she will ensure it in her own way," she said, and the two of them turned their focus to the tiny lights that beckoned them.

12

The Wedding

It would have been misleading to say that Paul awoke early the next morning; in truth, he did not sleep at all, and simply arose early, when he thought he might as well give up on getting any sleep. Marie had taken the night shift to watch Mukisa, telling him that he would have the rest of his life to spend the night with her daughter, so he had retreated to his own bed, after a few moments of conversation with his Mama and Wyatt. Now, he quietly put on some clothes, trying not to wake the two peaceful sleepers in their separate quarters.

He slowly inched open the door, stepped onto the threshold of the house, and promptly froze, his eyes becoming wide as saucers as he stared out at the morning sky.

Withdrawing into the house, he hurriedly closed the door, perhaps a little too loudly, and leaned up against it, his heart sinking.

The noise awoke Wyatt. He propped himself on his elbow, yawning and scratching his head, then focused in on Paul. He opened his mouth to give a congratulatory greeting, but faltered when he saw Paul's face. "What's the matter?"

Paul stared morosely down at him, not answering. He shuffled back into his room, and returned with his spear in hand. Wyatt's eyes bulged. "Seriously, what's going on?"

Paul opened the door and, still without a word, slipped outside, closing the door firmly behind him. Wyatt scrambled up and leapt for the door, a strange mix of panic and curiosity fueling his speed.

It was overcast, making them hard to see at first, but their movement gave them away, their wings hard at work in the lack of wind. It was more than Wyatt had ever seen — he did a quick head count, and lost track at thirty. A soft moan slipped from his mouth, and he grabbed the doorway to support himself.

There were a few specters perching on the houses closest to the field, and Paul approached them with a determined air. He thrust the spear towards them as they screeched and flew upwards. "*Get away!*" he screamed, chasing after them a little until they finally flew off into the sky.

He swung around and zeroed in on another small knot of specters, sitting on the clotheslines on the green. They eyed him, and took off as soon as he started towards them, clearly not too keen on having a confrontation with his spear.

"Paul."

Paul whirled around, his eyes landing on Chancellor. He stood before him with a somber look on his face, almost apologetic. Paul stared at him, breathing heavily, his mind racing. Chancellor's face was worn, his eyes puffy with exhaustion. He had been digging again. "Have they been here all night?"

"They started showing up about an hour ago. They apparently wake up earlier than we do."

Wyatt dashed over, apparently having found his strength. "How can there be so many?!" he cried, craning his neck upwards.

Chancellor turned to stare out at the field. "The field is a jealous Mother."

"I think she's being a little too jealous," Wyatt gulped.

Chancellor ignored him, placing his hand gently on Paul's shoulder. "I'm sorry, son. I don't think you're going to have your wedding today."

Paul clenched his fists tightly around his spear, a resolute glint in his eyes. "Day's just begun. They have until the afternoon to clear out."

"I don't think—"

"I'll stab every one of them if I have to, Sheriff. We're getting married today."

"Well, if you get to stab a specter, I want a chance, too," a voice said behind them. Paul smiled, and they turned to see Mukisa, a sly grin on her face, with one of her favorite knives in hand.

Wyatt laughed. "Not your average pre-wedding ritual, but go for it." He held up his hands. "Me, I'm gonna stick to gardening."

And so Chancellor and Wyatt set to work helping the Southern Village get their daily routines done; and Paul and Mukisa continued to guard the village for the rest of the morning: running at the beasts and brandishing their weapons, letting out yells to scare them off.

At around noon, Mama Nina came to watch. She sidled up beside Mukisa after she had taken a particularly fierce charge.

"Fighting so close to your wedding," she murmured, her hands folded neatly in front of her.

Mukisa shrugged. "I think it's fitting. After all, Paul and I met while we were hunting in the forest, didn't we?" She winked at Paul.

"Perhaps it would be wise to rest before the ceremony."

Mukisa rolled her eyes. "If we don't get them out of here, there won't *be* a ceremony."

And with that, she flung her knife at the nearest cluster of specters, several yards away.

Unexpectedly, the knife struck one of them, right in the gut, and it fell to the ground with a terrible shriek. This hit startled Mukisa just as much as it did the other specters, who split off into the air with their own piercing cries.

"Wow," Paul whispered, eyes wide. Behind him, Mama Nina stared in shock.

The specter lay still on the ground. Mukisa craned her neck, scared to move toward it. "Is it still alive?"

"It's still glowing," Paul said dubiously, though none of them were sure if that meant anything. They'd never seen a dead specter.

Mukisa quickly realized that this last victory had cleared out the rest of the specters from the village. They were, however, still perched within the trees at the border of the forest. They began to shriek, as though calling out to their dying friend. Mukisa shivered.

After a few moments, the specter's faint glow faded away, the last synapses firing through its veins.

Emboldened by this sign, Mukisa marched up to the carcass. A chill spread through her as she stooped to pull her knife from its gut, and her hand hesitated on the hilt. She had never gotten the chance to see a specter up close, in such detail. Its enormous wings lay haphazardly, the once taut skin now in loose disarray. It was the size of a small child; the muscles rippling under its skin indicated years of life, and yet... it was unnerving to see how many characteristics the creature shared with that of a human child, especially in its face. In fact, no longer embracing a snarl, the specter looked so innocent; with the glow gone from its skin, it took Mukisa all of her focus to remember that she had just killed a beast.

But it *was* just a beast, wasn't it? Mukisa's heart began to pound in her chest. She closed her eyes for a brief moment, and Martin's red eyes flashed before her, Wyatt's words echoing in her mind — *its eyes glowed red*. Her hand, still wrapped around the hilt of the knife, began to shake, and she ripped it from the flesh, her breathing becoming shallow, her vision sliding out of focus.

No. She caught her breath. This was a specter — not a human child, no matter how much it looked like one — she would do well to remember that. And yet—

"Is it dead?" Paul called out, and Mukisa jolted back to reality. She nudged it with her foot, and let out her breath long and slow, shutting out the odd feeling that had come upon her. Yes, dead. A dead animal — one that continually desired to harm her people. She was glad it lay dead before her.

She glanced over at where Paul and Mama Nina stood, and noticed that she had drawn the attention of many of the other villagers. She smiled. "Guess we'll finally get to try specter meat on our wedding day."

"No!" Mama Nina's voice came suddenly and firmly. The old woman strode forward with surprising urgency and knelt by the carcass, studying it shrewdly. After a moment, she turned her face toward Mukisa, who still held her knife. She gave her a sad smile — Mukisa couldn't quite understand the turmoil behind it — and took the dead specter in her arms, slowly moving with it toward the forest.

"Mama, where are you going?" Paul called after her. She made no reply, and Mukisa's stomach turned a little as she tried to blot the image of the specter's face from her mind.

The village watched as Mama Nina reached the edge of the forest, stepped carefully past the fence, and laid the specter at the foot of a tree.

Then she slowly made her way back to the crowd of onlookers. "No one will touch that body," she stated, looking around at the villagers.

Mukisa swallowed, fighting the feel of bile rising in her throat. *Get yourself under control, Mukisa.* "Why? These beasts have attacked us before, they've pushed our loved ones under the mud... and you're suddenly trying to, what, give them some respect?"

Mama gave her a level stare. "You don't have to give them respect, child. But you will not touch that body."

Mukisa narrowed her eyes. "But *why*?" she repeated.

Mama suddenly looked very tired. She hesitated for a moment, then sighed. "Because I said so, Mukisa." She presented herself to the

234

rest of the crowd. "Would anyone like to question my wisdom on this matter?"

No one spoke. In that moment, Mama seemed so frail and upset that Mukisa was sure the village would have made oaths of silence if it meant she'd feel better.

She rolled her eyes. It didn't matter... she realized, as she looked at the position of the sun in the sky, that it was time for her to get ready.

Her mother waited for her at the Guest House, the cloth folded neatly in her arms. Now freed of the dirt that had previously weighed it down, it was soft and pliable, and a creamy white.

Marie wrapped the fabric around Mukisa, pinning one end here and tucking in the corners there, and an hour later, Mukisa was spinning around the room, grinning to herself and holding up the train of the dress as she watched the material move with her.

She smiled as she glanced out the window at the bustling village. "Beautiful dress... one less specter to deal with..." She turned to her mother, the very image of a beaming bride. "This wedding is looking out to be pretty wonderful."

She was too busy twirling around in her new dress to see the specters come for the body; they came to the edge of the forest, letting out soft cries of distress. Their hands pleaded with their cold friend, searching for a sign of life; and when a few moments' time were unable to bring forth such a sign, the creatures collected their lost companion, taking flight and disappearing into the dark of the forest.

♦

The village gathered just before twilight, clutching jars full of fireflies that had not yet begun to blink and glow.

Standing to the side of the crowd, Chancellor could not stop fidgeting. Getting married was nerve-wracking enough; watching your daughter get married was a completely different animal. Beside him, Marie stared up at the sky, the look of worry never leaving her face.

"It'll be fine," Chancellor murmured, wondering as he spoke the words if they were for Marie or for himself. "The specters have gone. They'll be fine."

The legions of specters had, indeed, melted away, but Marie shook her head. "They're *all* gone," she muttered under her breath. "Why are they *all* gone? Doesn't that seem suspicious to you? There are usually at least a couple in the sky, up until the sun completely disappears… and compared to this morning, we now see none? Especially after what happened…"

Chancellor followed her gaze to the sky. It was true: there was not a single specter in sight. He studied Marie's face silently for a moment. "You don't always need to worry, you know. Sometimes things work out. Just because they didn't for us—"

"Chancellor, now is *not* the time."

"Look, I'm just saying… your daughter is about to get married, and all you can think about is whether or not the specters are going to appear. You can't accept that things will go smoothly, can you? You expect the worst because the worst happened to you, but that kind of thinking will ruin this experience for you. It'll be fine, Marie. Enjoy our daughter's day."

Marie took a deep breath and nodded. She glanced out across the field and smiled. "There he is."

Chancellor turned to see Paul standing at the opposite end of the field. He was clearly nervous; he kept adjusting his weight back and forth between his feet, and Chancellor recognized that he had stuffed his hands into his pockets to keep them from fidgeting.

Marie smiled at Paul's figure in the distance. She had watched him grow into such a smart, thoughtful, caring man. She never would have thought that the little boy who wriggled out of the mud twenty-three years ago would be the one who united with her daughter, but she was glad for it to happen. She glanced over at Paul's mother, who stood with Wyatt, happy tears welling up in her eyes as Wyatt put his arm around her.

She felt a nudge on her shoulder, and

turned to see her daughter, a grin broken out on her face. Her dress flowed to the ground, the cloth trailing out behind her. "I'm ready, Mama."

"Are you sure...?"

Mukisa pulled back one of the folds in her dress, revealing one of her knives. "To keep the specters in line."

Marie gave a sigh of relief. Then she embraced her daughter tightly, fighting back tears. She felt her daughter holding the embrace a little longer than normal. "You let yourself cry, now, Mama," she whispered. "No wearing your mask on my wedding day."

Marie laughed and let a few tears start to trickle down. She could allow that, she supposed.

Mukisa pulled away, smiling, and turned to her father. "Daddy?"

Chancellor beamed and pulled her in. Stiff at first from the surprise of the embrace, she finally relaxed, and when they released each other, Mukisa did her best to hide her fluster.

The light from the jars began to twinkle in the growing darkness; later, the fireflies would be released as the couple had their first dance, but for now, they jostled the glass, sending soft pricks of light into the approaching dusk. Mukisa made her way to the foot of the field, and turned to stare out at her people.

Mama Nina stepped forward, helping Mukisa spread the train of the dress out on the ground, then gently touched her shoulder and gave her a warm smile. She turned to address the crowd. "You all know how this works. Please, one at a time."

And so, one by one, each villager approached the bride, squatting carefully and submerging a hand into the shallow edges of the field, pulling their hand out and pressing it into the fabric of Mukisa's dress. The adults helped the youngest, making sure they did not spread the mud around too much, so that there would be room for everyone. Even John and Wyatt added their handprints to the cloth. Slowly, the garment began to fade into the field around it, the mud extending all the way up to Mukisa's waist.

Mukisa beamed as the villagers finished their work. Glancing out across the field, she caught Paul's eye. She winked, and saw him laugh.

As the last of the villagers made their mark on the cloth, Mama Nina again stepped forward and took her hand, addressing the crowd once more. "Though this child had origins other than the depths of the field," she began, nodding toward Chancellor and Marie, "the message remains the same: from where we came, from which we celebrate our ties. Let this field be the symbol of a love grown strong, of a unity marked by those who promise to uphold it and feed it with support." She turned to face Mukisa, squeezing her hand. "And now, let the two lovers unite!"

Mukisa laughed, unable to stop herself. The villagers cheered; Chancellor and Marie clasped hands in the anonymity of the crowd, the folds of Marie's dress obscuring the moment.

Mukisa stepped out onto the field, the train of the dress trailing behind her; across the way, Paul did the same. Both held their breath as they drew closer and closer, making the trek that seemed to take forever; they finally met in the middle of the field and grasped hands, intertwining their fingers and staring into each other's eyes.

"You got a little dirt on you," Paul whispered, and Mukisa gave his hands a little shake, a smile peeking through her mock scowl. Behind her, she heard cheers erupt once more.

But their cheers quickly faded as the field around the couple began to bubble. The two lovers stared down in horror at the mud, then up at each other, panic beginning to set in as the ground beneath them began to shift.

From the forest, the specters began to emerge.

Mukisa turned to see her mother rushing toward the field; but the mud was already bubbling dangerously across its entirety, and she hesitated at the edge. "Get off the field!" she yelled. Mukisa was not about to disobey her mother on this matter. She prodded Paul forward, and they charged away from the center of the field, hand in hand, Mukisa holding the train of her dress in a bunch to keep from tripping.

Unfortunately, the dress was quite lengthy, the cloth being meant to fit any shape or size, and inevitably, less than a second of running caused Mukisa's foot to snag on the end of the cloth. She toppled to the ground, and Paul doubled back, still grasping her hand.

Mukisa let out a small moan of fear as Paul stooped forward to help her. "Come on!" he cried frantically. She grabbed onto his shoulders and staggered to her feet, her heart slamming viciously into her ribcage like a trapped animal.

The mud was now rolling across the field like waves, and they did their best to hurdle over it. Paul yelled as a horde of specters came out of the trees in a swarm, zigzagging towards them, claws outstretched. He waved his free arm at them, trying to scare them off.

Mukisa gasped as one looming wave crashed into them from behind, buckling their knees and catapulting them to the ground. She put both hands out in front of her in anticipation, but her face still hit the mud, and her feet slid as she tried to stand back up. She felt the mud oozing through her fingers, and her heart dropped into her stomach as she realized she had lost hold of Paul's hand.

She whipped her head around. Paul was already receding into the mud, struggling, eyes wide with fear as the specters swooped in on them.

Mukisa screamed as she felt the wings fall on her, dealing heavy blows to her back and face. She grabbed the knife from her waist and swung her arm out, the blade connecting with one specter, then two. But there were too many of them; she was fighting her way over to Paul, but it was happening too slowly.

She sliced her knife into a specter's wing, and the creature hissed and swooped forward, knocking Mukisa back. It splayed its talons toward her, its childlike face leering down at her, and Mukisa felt a lurch of nausea at the humanity in its snarl. She quickly rolled out of the way as it attacked, and crashed into another specter, wings beating and talons poised — its face floated inches from hers, its eyes carving their way into her mind.

She cried out and shoved herself through the barrage of claws and wings, finally inching herself forward enough. Paul reached for her desperately; she flung herself toward him, and their fingers connected for one split second, but another wave of mud pummeled them, completely engulfing Paul and knocking Mukisa backwards.

Mukisa gasped and landed on her back, momentarily stunned. The mud around her instantly stilled, and the air filled with the shrieks of the specters as they suddenly began to lift off into the sky, departing. She bolted back up, and searched the mud in front of her frantically for Paul.

She found nothing. She could not see him.

Mukisa let out a deep, anguished howl

and plunged her arms into the mud around her. She sifted through the mud, reaching in as far as her shoulders, pushing back her scraggly hair with mud-caked hands, digging into the soil relentlessly, nearly choking on her own spit.

She heard hurried footsteps behind her, and felt hands on her shoulders, felt herself being hoisted up into the air, heard grunts as she lashed out. She let out scream after scream, a siren to call her husband home.

13

The Plan

Mukisa was confined to her house.

People came to visit; or at least they said they were visiting. But she knew; she could hear them whispering to each other in the door frame, prodding each other to take up the next shift — there was always at least one person with her at all times, in keeping with her mother's heightened watch. But no matter how many people came to see her, Mukisa was still beside herself.

At first, with each visitor, she had tried to find a way to sneak out of her confinement, determined to go back to the field. The villagers had resisted her pleading and cajoling and sometimes even had to call for reinforcements as she occasionally attempted to strong-arm her way through the door. This continued until the day after the fall, when Mama Nina came quietly into the room while Mukisa was having another tantrum, dismissed the guard, and sat, her stare stern and resolute, until Mukisa, fuming, sat on her bed and stared back.

"You must stop wasting your energy," Mama Nina said after a long moment. "What's done is done, child."

The statement simply made Mukisa angrier. "I am imprisoned in my own house," she replied darkly. "My sister and husband are imprisoned by the field. And this entire village is imprisoned by the fear brought on by the specters. And the specters! Mama..." She squeezed her eyes shut for a moment, taking a deep breath. "Mama, I think there's something wrong with the field, I think the field is doing things to us. I don't know why, but I... Martin, Mama. He had red eyes, before his fall... I didn't say anything, but I saw... I think it did something to him, Mama. And I don't think the specters are what we thought they are."

She opened her eyes to see Mama Nina's reaction. The woman was not surprised. Mukisa sighed. "You know what's going on, don't you?"

She was silent for a moment. "I have known for a while now."

Mukisa jumped to her feet. "Then how

can you keep me locked in here, when you and I both know that the people under that field are going to be changed? Transformed into beasts? Mother Mud is destroying her children, and making them like the specters!"

Mama Nina gave her a weary, almost disappointed look. "Sit, child." She sighed and folded her hands neatly in her lap. "You're going to do some serious thinking about what has happened."

Mukisa blinked. "So you're accusing me—"

"I am presenting your situation to you. I cannot control your actions, but I can at least give you some perspective."

"*I have perspective!*" Mukisa spat.

Mama Nina gazed levelly at her. "There are many ways to look at a situation, Mukisa. Just because your perspective changes does not mean you see the picture fully." Mukisa grimaced and sat, and the old woman continued. "So. What has happened?" Mukisa remained sulkily silent, and Mama leaned forward. "Tell me."

Mukisa scrutinized Mama Nina for a moment. She was acting oddly. How could she be so calm? How could she know what the field was doing, and be so calm? It couldn't be to soothe her — no, with this knowledge, Mukisa couldn't be soothed.

But it seemed that Mama had in mind another one of her lessons — she asked a question in order to transport Mukisa to a specific stream of thought. She rolled her eyes and submitted. "I pushed my betrothed to his own fall." A wave of emotions hit her with those words; her mind buzzed and her chest heaved, and she closed her eyes for a moment — and then she was fine, pushing her emotions to the corner.

She regathered her thoughts, and focused on the old woman before her, who had a reproachful look on her face. She thought for a moment. "Maybe I didn't push him under *physically*," she corrected herself, "but he wouldn't have fallen under if it weren't for me. He didn't want to rush the wedding. But I thought... and I killed the specter... they should have gone after me!" The panic returned, and she looked pleadingly at the old woman. "Why didn't they go after me, Mama? I'm the one who killed one of them — oh, Mama, if it's true, maybe I killed one of *us* — I'm the one who deserved the mud, not him..."

And then came the question, the question that she had been waiting to ask for so long but hadn't realized how to form it into words. "I'm different, aren't I, Mama?"

Mama remained calm, in stark contrast to the tears now streaming down Mukisa's face. "Everyone's different, child. You'll have to be more specific."

Mukisa thought for a moment, piecing together her thoughts. "Martin. He was affected by the field. He spent so long under the mud, it started to change him into something he was not, and that's why he was becoming so nasty and ill-tempered — he was becoming like a specter. But before he fell back under... he said that he and I were a lot alike. But he got that way because of what the field did to him!" She sighed. "What the hell is my excuse?"

Mama searched her eyes. "That doesn't mean you're different. I feel that way sometimes, too."

"What do you mean?"

"I think we are all more like Martin than we realize. Deep down." Mama smiled. "But some of us haven't had the reason to reach that far inside ourselves, to see what we are. You, Mukisa... these past few years have given you more than enough of a reason to wear your heart on your sleeve. And Martin... well, you're right. The field changed him; but it didn't change him into another person. It just... brought his true self to the surface."

Mukisa stared at her. "Well, that's a bit of a defeatist view."

Mama simply shrugged.

Mukisa frowned and shook her head, trying to organize her thoughts. "I don't know, I think it happened to my grandfather too. My mother said the field changed him — that her mother never really got her husband back from the mud, that he had transformed into a mean, nasty beast." She sighed in frustration. "What is making the field do this to us?"

The shade of solemnity fell back over Mama Nina's face. "Let's return to the events on the field."

Mukisa gave her an impatient look. "Why do you want so badly for me to think about what happened on the field?"

Mama gazed at her steadily. "So that you understand the consequences."

Mukisa narrowed her eyes. Well, she didn't know what that was supposed to mean. "The consequences are simple," she said. "I caused mayhem. I forced a wedding upon the village, at a time like this. Mayhem. Just like the mayhem I forced on the village five years ago."

Mama clucked disapprovingly. "Always stuck in the past," she murmured. "You didn't force mayhem on the village. You defended your family, and the village built mayhem around your defense."

Mukisa glared at her. "But I was the one who started it. I killed a man, Mama! My own kin."

"He was still alive when he went under," Mama said softly.

Mukisa was sure her tone was meant to appease her — it wasn't her fault. She didn't kill him. If he died while under the mud, well, that was the fault of the field, wasn't it? She grimaced. "So I did something even worse than murder. I threw a man into hell."

"He was already in hell." Mukisa blinked; she had expected admonition for calling the field a place of hell. But Mama had a different train of thought. A strange look crossed her face. "Perhaps you even saved him from it."

"I saved him from *nothing*." Mukisa cradled her head in her hands. "I did to him what he would have done to me. Given his history, that's about as far from salvation as you can get. I'm turning into him." She laughed darkly. "And he was turning into something else. How's that for irony… the field never got a hold of me, but that damn man did. He made sure to pass his legacy on through hate… so I still act like a specter, after all."

But Mama, who was looking at Mukisa with a doleful expression, did not laugh. "No," she said simply. "There's hope for you yet." She gave a small smile. "Your saving grace is the decision you made years ago, child."

"What, to kill?" Mukisa shot back.

"To stand up for what is right," Mama said softly, her kind eyes locking with Mukisa's. "And to this day, you have continued to do just that."

She stood, and reached for the door. Once there, she hesitated, then turned to look Mukisa in the eyes. "You asked why the field was doing this to us." She smiled sadly. "It's a field, child. It doesn't do what it does out of spite. It just does what it's always done — it's never wavered from its course. We are the ones who waver."

She left her then, and her previous guard

returned to his spot, nervously glancing at her. His concern was unnecessary: Mukisa was done fighting for the night. She simply sat cross-legged on her bed and stared blankly at the wall, staying eerily quiet.

Something didn't feel right. Well — of course something didn't feel right. She was sitting by as the field went to work on her loved ones, sprouting wings from their backs and fangs from their teeth and anger in their hearts. How long would it take? How long, really, did she have before she would lose her family forever to an unstable, misbehaving field? And why?

But there was still something nagging in the back of her mind. Something that Mama Nina clearly knew; why she wanted to keep it a secret was beyond her comprehension. If anything, she should tell anyone who would listen about what was happening under the fields.

And yet Mukisa could not bring herself to tell anyone but Mama what she had learned. Why? What was holding *her* back? Again, that nagging. What was that one last missing piece — the full picture that Mama had referred to?

"We are the ones who waver." The woman was infuriating. If she could just come out and say what she meant, then maybe this wouldn't all be so confusing. Who was "we" — the village? How was the village wavering? The village was the embodiment of stagnation. The

villagers had been doing the same thing for years upon years: life was broken down into a mere handful of activities. The village had been the absolute *opposite* of "wavering" since... well, if Mukisa could take a guess, since the First Man emerged from the field.

Mukisa felt a cold sweep through her, her heart jumping into her throat as the pieces began clicking into place one by one. *"We are the ones who waver."* The ones who clambered out of the mud, not by strength of their own but through the strength of those who came before. *"We are the ones who waver."* The ones with the guilty consciences, the ones whose choice was either to dig or to sentence others to what was assumed to be a lifetime under the field. But would it be a lifetime?

"No, no, no, no, no," she cried, her eyes widening. The guard across the room nearly jumped out of his skin at the sudden outburst, and Mukisa clasped her hands over her mouth, her head spinning. She turned her gaze resolutely to the guard. "I want Wyatt Pine to take the next shift," she blurted out.

The guard gave her a panicked look; but he quickly stuck his head out through the doorway; and sure enough, when the time came to change guards, Wyatt Pine sat awkwardly in the seat before her.

By that point, Mukisa had resumed her silence. Her body was still, but her mind was racing. She didn't look at Wyatt during the first hour; she didn't have to. She knew he would be fidgeting, sitting in the corner and eyeing her nervously. He was not up to the job of guarding her. This was part of why she had asked him to come.

She tried to gather her thoughts. She had a plan, of sorts, but she wondered if her mind was now too numb to carry it out. Now that she had exhausted herself with her thoughts, it was hard enough to put the room in focus, let alone organize her escape.

But she had to escape — that desire had only been escalated from Mama Nina's little talk. Otherwise she would be stuck in here with her new realization, a realization she was sure would ruin her. The impact of her discovery would press in on her mind, make it collapse and dissolve into itself. Strange how just an hour ago, there had been two disconnected visions in her mind: the field as a womb, and the field as a monster, transforming its prisoners. Like it had gone rogue. But now those visions were colliding. No, not colliding — embracing. It wasn't what the people under the mud were becoming — it was what they *were*. Maybe even what *she* was. She pushed that last realization from her mind — one chaotic thought at a time. What she needed to focus on now was the field; she couldn't let that cycle become complete. She could *not* let her family meet that destiny.

"What did you see under the mud?" she asked suddenly.

Wyatt jumped at the sudden interaction.

He swallowed nervously. "I saw a specter—"

"No. What else did you see?"

Wyatt narrowed his eyes. "What do you mean?"

"Was there anything else down there? Did you see *anything* other than the specter? Just… tell me what you saw."

Wyatt sighed. "I saw bodies. I saw comatose bodies."

"How did you see the bodies? I mean… if you were surrounded by mud."

"Once I got a certain distance down from the surface of the field, the mud gave way to water. Or not water… I don't know what it was. But it was liquid. And I could breathe it in, whatever it was. And it was clear, I could see all around me."

Mukisa leaned forward, paying rapt attention now. "And they were unconscious?" He nodded, and Mukisa's gaze drifted.

Wyatt shrugged. "I felt completely drained when I resurfaced… maybe just being under the mud knocks you out."

"You felt drained — from terror? Exertion?"

Wyatt thought about that for a moment. "No… I don't think that's it. I didn't feel scared down there; not until the specter showed up. I felt… I don't know, it was kind of nice. I felt… like I was supposed to be there. It was inviting, and calming. I could've been lulled to sleep if I had stayed under any longer." He laughed. "That's Mother Mud, making me feel right at home."

Mukisa felt the hair on the back of her neck stand straight up. She resisted the urge to ask the question that was on her mind — "How long was it before you felt drained?" — knowing that this would only arouse suspicion. Instead, she quickly plopped down in her bed, rolling to face the wall so that Wyatt could not see her expression.

But she was glad she had questioned him. He had reminded her of one important thing that had somehow slipped her mind: the specter. That was an obstacle she would have to overcome. It must be Martin, she thought suddenly. He'd had the red eyes, and he had certainly spent enough time under the mud.

And so the next couple of hours went: Mukisa pretended to be asleep, when in fact she was wide awake and listening, waiting, her brain churning.

About halfway through the night, she chanced a look and noticed that Wyatt's eyes were closed. She smiled. He had made the perfect watch guard — the kind that fell asleep on the job. Exactly what she had been hoping for. She slowly crawled out of bed, keeping her eyes on him the entire time, and inched the door open, sneaking out into the night before he even stirred. Closing the door behind her, she stared out into the darkness, waiting for her eyes to adjust.

If they were going to watch her every waking moment, then she was going to make the best of the moments that no one was awake. Mama Nina was right: she couldn't control Mukisa's actions — but she had known exactly what her plans were. Whether she could see the "full picture" or not, the solution was still the same: she wouldn't allow her family to stay trapped under the mud.

She approached the field slowly. There was no lantern lying around for her to use today, and she looked up at the sky, nodding an appreciative thank you to the full moon that lit her way.

But the moon was not bright enough to reveal Chancellor's frame in the shadows. He stepped out as she reached the field and cleared his throat. "Don't do this, Mukisa."

Mukisa spun around and found him in the moonlight. Her face filled with despair. "Why are you lurking?!" she yelled.

"Mukisa, your volume," Chancellor murmured, approaching her.

"I don't care about my volume. Just leave me alone!"

Chancellor reached her and held out his hands in an attempt to show he came in peace. She laughed darkly and took a step back, and Chancellor quickly grabbed her arm and pulled her forward again, preventing her from stepping onto the field. "*No*," he said firmly. "You are not going back out there."

"Like hell I'm not."

He let out a sigh of frustration. "You will be in danger as soon as you step out on that field. Why don't you understand that?"

Mukisa clenched her fists. "I do understand it. But sometimes danger is worth the risk, to save your loved ones."

"Mukisa…"

"Let me go! *Let me go*!"

The commotion caused several doors to open, the villagers inside peering out curiously. Wyatt was one of them, throwing the door to Mukisa's home open in panicked guilt.

Mukisa shook herself away from Chancellor's grip, and turned to look in horror at her new audience. She shot a reproachful glance at her father.

The door to the Guest House opened, and Marie stepped out. "What's going on here?" Tears came to Mukisa's eyes. Marie approached, shaking her head, and placed her hand on her daughter's shoulder. "Come on, Mukisa. Let's get back to bed."

"Mama, I'm not going back to bed! This has gone on long enough!" Mukisa let out a determined sigh. She couldn't explain what she had come to understand, but she could at least explain her intentions. "I want to go under, Mama."

Marie stared in shock at her child. "What?"

"I want to go under, to save Paul, to save Cecilia. I want to try to uproot the specter under the mud."

"Mukisa, think about what you're saying," Chancellor spoke up, his face lined with fear.

"You won't be able to control what happens to you once you are under the field. Otherwise no one would stay under there."

"Wyatt was able to control it!" Mukisa shot back. From his spot in the doorway, Wyatt's face blanched.

"Wyatt was able to remember a few seconds under the field," Marie said. "That doesn't mean he had control. And that doesn't mean you would be able to remain conscious if you went under yourself. You'll be lost under there, and we'll never be able to get you back, and then you'll be causing the very thing you wanted to prevent."

Mukisa's mind was racing even faster now. "Then I'll tie a rope around me," she replied, "and you can hold onto the other end, and pull me up when you get worried."

"I'm already worried."

"Mama, you've got to at least give me a chance," Mukisa whispered, stepping towards her hopefully. "If no one else is going to do anything, at least let me try."

"I'll go with you."

Mukisa turned to see her father stepping forward, coming up beside her. He took her hand and squeezed it lovingly, and she smiled at him, feeling a twinge of hope.

Marie let out a frustrated sigh, shaking her head. "Chancellor, what are you doing?"

"She's right, Marie. We've been taking passive measures, but we've got to be more active with this beast. Otherwise it's just going to keep pushing us around. You've seen the specters lately... and they don't look like they're going to relent any time soon. But maybe they would if their friend wasn't down there."

Marie closed her eyes for a moment. She murmured something which was hard to make out, but Mukisa felt she heard the word "insane" in its midst.

Wyatt stumbled out of his doorway and ran to stand beside Mukisa and Chancellor. "I'll go too," he said breathlessly. Amongst the villagers, John was heard letting out a string of curses under his breath.

The villagers began to whisper to each other, eyes wide. Marie glanced around at the commotion, then glared at her daughter. "Don't do this," she begged, holding back tears. "Don't you dare start a revolution based on madness."

"It's not a revolution if the whole village agrees to it," Mukisa whispered. And it was as she said: several villagers were slowly coming from their homes, walking towards them. They passed Marie and stood beside her daughter, lining up in front of the field resolutely.

◆

The next day, the village worked together to make the strongest rope they could for "The Big Fall", as they had begun to call it. Marie was extremely displeased with this new nickname, and refused to help them in their

259

mission; but her views on the matter were, surprisingly enough, suddenly the rarity in the village. Though she tried to enforce that everyone continue the jobs that they were assigned to, like they did every day, many — some gardeners, soap makers, those on the building committee — still decided to skip out for the day, searching for materials instead.

By noon, enough rope had been gathered to begin piecing together, and the villagers set avidly to work. John plopped himself onto the ground beside Wyatt, reaching for a piece of rope and beginning to unravel one end, in order to twine it together with the next piece. "So I hope you've figured out," he said slowly, concentrating hard on the work before him, "that I can't just let you go under the field without me."

Wyatt did not reply at first; but after a moment, he glanced at him, suddenly realizing what John's words meant. "Does... does that mean you're coming too?"

John scowled for a moment. "Yeah, I reckon it does."

Wyatt beamed, and threw his arms around him, an action which John quickly tried to deter. "No— what are you doing?!" he cried, flustered. "That's no reason to be happy! You — you should be very ashamed of the fact that you're putting me in danger right alongside you!"

Wyatt suppressed his grin and returned

to his work, altogether much more confident in the mission.

That brought the count to four people who were willing to go under. Before they were even finished with their work, several other villagers volunteered to hold the ropes when they were under the mud, which was just as important a job, if they were ever planning on resurfacing without any hitches. They assigned four people per rope, just in case any problems arose.

Mukisa sat a distance away from the other villagers, working on a piece of rope. Coming up beside her, Mama Nina eased herself onto the ground into a kneeling position. The position looked entirely uncomfortable for such an old woman. "Feeling sorry for yourself?" she asked.

Mukisa gave her a sharp look. "What do you mean?"

"You are not working near the others. There must be a reason you're keeping yourself in isolation."

She heaved a sigh. "They'd rather I keep my distance."

Mama Nina was silent, staring at Mukisa as she twisted the strands of rope together. It was a searching stare, as she sifted through the emotions that fleetingly crossed Mukisa's face. The old woman always knew, didn't she? Mukisa sighed. "I understand the consequences."

The old woman raised an eyebrow. "Oh?"

"I figured it out after you talked to me.

How have you kept it a secret—?"

"Hush, child." Mama hesitated for a moment, pondering the question. "Truthfully, it hasn't been that difficult. I like to think that my years in this village have given me the wisdom to see things more clearly. Not to mention, I remembered my nightmares. The idea that this," she said in a low tone, glancing out at the field, "had happened before was not so crazy to me. This is not the only time that the specters have been drawn to the field in hordes — they come to collect. But other times, people didn't notice. This time, we are on our guard." She smiled at Mukisa. "I have always been on my guard. You see, we are a strange people. We're always searching for some kind of truth… always questioning, but never truly listening for an answer. I, on the other hand, sometimes have the curse of discovering those answers."

"How is it a curse, if you were looking for it in the first place?"

There was a knowing glint in Mama Nina's eyes. "What a good question," she said. "Do you feel blessed by the knowledge you now have?" Mukisa didn't answer, and Mama Nina patted her hand. "Or here's a better one: if you think the village wants nothing to do with you, then why do you think they're helping you?"

Mukisa frowned, finding herself at a loss for words as Mama slowly got to her feet and ambled away.

Within a couple of hours, the four ropes

had been created, strong enough to hold enough weight, and long enough that they could go a speculative ten yards under the surface of the field.

Mukisa saw her mother watching them tensely as they gathered near the field, double-checking their materials and manpower. Each volunteer slid a weapon into their belt: for Mukisa, it was her knife; for Chancellor, it was one of the axes used by the building committee for chopping wood; John had his trusty shovel; and Wyatt had borrowed a spear from Paul's collection.

And then it was time. The village gathered around the four volunteers, their faces full of nervous anticipation.

There was one last thing to do before they began their journey under the mud. Mukisa approached her mother, a question in her eyes. "Mama... please be okay with this."

"How could I ever be okay with this?"

"But you must be somewhat okay with it. You're letting us go."

"I am letting you go because you are very much your father's daughter... nothing will sway your mind. But that doesn't mean I have to be happy about it. If you wanted to submit me to this endless worry, then you're making the right move."

"Then come with us," Mukisa suggested, knowing she was taking a stab in the dark. The reply was a cold glare.

Chancellor stepped forward, putting his

hand on Marie's shoulder. "We'll be stronger with you, Marie," he whispered.

Marie glared fiercely at him. "No."

"I'll be stronger with you."

Marie avoided eye contact, her eyes sliding out of focus. "You proved that wrong five years ago on the day you left."

Chancellor's hand fell weakly from her shoulder. Mukisa gave Chancellor a meaningful look as they stepped back in line with John and Wyatt. She ventured one more glance at her mother. "We'll be back," she said feebly, and turned toward the mud; before her line of view had completely passed her mother, however, she noticed the shaking hands and felt her heart get a little bit heavier.

The four of them made their way onto the field, holding tightly to their ropes, and stopped a good portion of the way in. Mukisa faced them, motioning for them to tie their ropes onto themselves. "All right. We'll all go in together. If you see the specter, yell. If you hear someone yelling, go toward the sound."

"How can we yell under the mud?" Chancellor asked.

Wyatt gave him a nervous shrug. "It's possible, trust me."

"One more thing," Mukisa said, taking a deep breath and staring at each of them in turn. "We may see loved ones down there, people who have fallen under. If you can, grab them and we'll bring them back. But if the specter's anywhere in sight… we'll deal with the specter first, and we can always go back later."

"What if we can't kill it?" Wyatt said shakily. "What if it's too strong?"

Mukisa hesitated, suddenly understanding why Mama Nina had been so adamant about respecting the dead specter's body the other day. She hadn't thought ahead so far as to what they would actually do to the specter. *Should* they kill it? That was just like killing one of their own. It *was* one of their own.

But she couldn't explain that to them. She couldn't lay down the implications of going after the specter under the mud, for the very reason that Mama Nina had been silent for all these years. She would have to do a secretly dirty deed in order to keep the people's peace of mind. She sighed. "It will be strong," she said, "But it will be alone." I hope, she thought. "We have strength in our numbers."

The thought seemed to appease Wyatt, at least for the moment. Mukisa tugged on the rope around her waist, checking the knot. "Are we ready?"

One by one, they nodded somberly.

"Then let's go."

Mukisa sucked in a deep breath, her heart pounding in her chest. This was it. She watched her father kneel in the mud and drop forward, sinking down and out of sight. She heard a sucking noise to her right, and watched Wyatt dive right under, as if he had been born to do so. On the other side of her, John grimaced and dug a little hole in front of him before somersaulting into the mess.

Mukisa glanced back at the people waiting at the edge of the field. The pullers were all in position, holding the ropes already just in case they were needed prematurely. Mukisa saw her mother, panic written across her face, and her heart gave a twinge at the sight. Right now, that woman felt as if she was alone in the world, and Mukisa knew there was a ridiculous notion of guilt being tossed around in that head of hers. That was Mama… she was the only person Mukisa knew who could blame herself for feeling too much. But she couldn't do anything about that now. It was time to go.

She turned away from the spectators and dove under.

14

The Return

Jezra sat before Marie, silent, staring at her and waiting patiently. Marie could not decide what emotions her eyes held: disappointment or regret. Either way, Marie did not feel comfortable with what the outcome of this conversation might be.

She looked different than she had when Marie had resided in the Northern Village. She was, after all, now the Sheriff — fifteen-plus years of being a deputy had paid off, but had certainly taken its toll. Those years had aged her significantly. Marie said a silent prayer, hoping that her disappearance hadn't added to her old friend's worry lines. If she could have explained to her why she had left, she *would have; but the older woman would have insisted that she stay to face her fears — they could have worked something out, they could always work something out. Marie had always wondered if the other villagers knew the reason she had departed anyway... but the look on Jezra's face said otherwise.*

"Adranna," she said gravely. "Please explain to me what is going on."

Marie fought to compose herself, the tears nearly on her cheeks. "I should've told you why I left," she began slowly. "I should have told someone. But I was too scared of what that man would do to me. No one knew what he did to me. And to Mama. I was scared..."

The tears began to fall, and she couldn't stop them. Jezra's expression changed, but it did not soften. "I meant today, Adranna. Your dismissal of our village fifteen years ago is not of concern to me at the moment. What I am concerned about is that there has been a death in our village, and it has been caused by one of your own."

The words stung. Of course Jezra didn't care about what had happened. Running away at the age of seventeen, after her mother had died no less... There was no way that it would look like a cry for help, only an act of rebellion. Anger boiled in Marie's chest. Papa had probably put up a big fuss, about how Adranna never respected him, and he was so sick with worry, and how could she do this to him? And how would the other villagers have known any better? He was so careful to never slip up, to keep the bruises and the tears hidden.

"What did you tell her about Calam?"

"What?"

"What did you tell your daughter, that she would commit such an act of violence?"

Marie's heart fell into her stomach. "My daughter was acting out of defense. I never told her anything but the truth about my father, and even then, it's not like I told her through bedtime stories every night. That is not a subject that I bring up lightly."

Jezra sighed. "I don't know what disagreements you had with Calam when you were still with us, Adranna, but I had hoped that you might not spread rumors about him still, to this day."

"To you, they may sound like rumors, Jezra; but to me, they were very real, and very—" She hesitated, taking a deep breath. "I would never wish my childhood on anyone, Jezra. Calam wanted to take my daughters with him, away from me. That is not acceptable."

"The question of custody does not permit murder, Adranna."

"It wasn't murder! It was self defense. My daughter is not a murderer."

"And yet she has murdered a man."

"There is no proof that he is dead."

Jezra gave her an exasperated glance, and Marie stared at the floor. Poor Mukisa. She had been ill since the accident, barely able to talk or move. She was in a state of shock, and rightly so. She had been protecting her family, and she had brought out the sparks; but her fire had caught a little too strongly this time, and Marie had no one to blame but herself. She should have spoken up, fifteen years ago, and then maybe things would be different… maybe the village would have recognized Calam's shameful acts, and done something about them. This was all her fault. This had happened because she had let it get this far.

"She's a child. She cannot be blamed."

"She is fourteen. More than enough of a woman to take responsibility for her actions. And you have her hunting in the woods, with spears and knives—"

"That's her job. Her contribution to society."

"Well. It's a bit barbaric. I can't say that I approve of a child doing an adult's work."

"Sounds to me like you can't decide if she's a woman or a child." Jezra gave her a sharp look. "Well, I guess if you don't approve… it's probably good that you don't have to raise her, then, isn't it?"

Jezra shot her a look of disapproval. "What has happened to you, Adranna? Who have you become? You used to be this shy, quiet little girl, always choosing to avoid conflict. And now you raise your daughters to use violence as a way of life. I'm sorry, Adranna, but—"

"Do not call me Adranna."

Jezra stared at her silently for a moment. "Mayor Kenton will be here shortly to take statements. He will be the one to decide what should be done, and do not think that he will have mercy for the one he finds at fault." She stood. "I would say it was nice to see you, but… given the circumstances…" She frowned, and left Marie to herself.

When Mayor Kenton did come, he ruled that Calam had been the instigator. It brought relief to Marie that his violence wasn't just her imagination, but she was sure that the Northern Village would cry foul. She expected they wouldn't like to see her any time soon, or anyone tied with the affair, for that matter. From here on out, the distrust between the villages would begin to grow.

It even affected Chancellor… Marie saw it in his eyes when he looked at his daughter, as she returned to her normal self and joined the rest of the community once more… there was something in the look he gave that could not be undone, something that had changed in the way he saw her. The sheriff of the Western Village came calling later that week, with the news that Chancellor's father had fallen ill… and when he left, Marie knew deep in her heart, even then, that he was not coming back.

◆

Marie stared out at the field as the volunteers dove under one by one. She was now losing another daughter to the field, and it was her fault. She should have prevented this from happening. What they were doing was impossible, they were going to get themselves killed or stuck under there somehow… and she could have stopped them. She could have locked them up, or she could have sent the Western Villagers home before any of this ridiculousness had begun. As the mud bubbled a bit from the disturbance of the volunteers, she felt the panic rising in her chest.

♦

Mukisa hurtled through yards of mud, her heart seizing in terror. Her nostrils filled with the oozing mess, and her ears clogged. Suddenly her head broke through and everything around her came flying into focus. She gasped, and sucked in clear blue water.

The sight was horrifyingly spectacular, and it took her a moment to catch her bearings. Around her, her comrades had already recuperated and were shimmying out of the wall of mud. She caught her father's eye as she broke free. Grinning, she gave him a thumbs-up and motioned for him to follow. Pushing herself forward, she kicked her feet, the others following in her wake. Together they swam away from the mud, their ropes still fastened to their bodies, sliding through the wall of mud as they went further and further down into the water.

The four of them circled together, looks of exhilaration on their faces. This underground ocean felt nurturing and inviting, just like Wyatt had described. Mukisa shuddered — given her bastard birth, never had the comparison of the field to a mother's womb felt like anything more than a comparison until now. The thought made her angry, and this emotion fueled her. She spun around, searching the water for the purpose of their mission, and everyone followed behind her.

But no specter was in sight. Just bodies, floating back and forth. Mukisa suddenly wanted to throw up. How had that not been the first thing she noticed? Everything Wyatt had told her seemed to be coming to life right before her eyes.

Focus, Mukisa, she thought, and scanned the endless blue before her. She motioned for everyone to spread out. The search was on.

Swimming further downward, Mukisa tried to relax her heart as bloated bodies drifted by her. The sight of them tipped her mind, and though she tried to adjust her thoughts to the mission before her, it was a struggle. She knew her main focus should be to look for the specter, but she could not help but search the face of every comatose body... how many people would she see before she recognized a face? How many people would she see before she found her sister and her husband?

And how was it that she was awake down in this blue ocean, but everyone around her was comatose? But even as she thought this, she felt her eyelids growing heavy. An alarm went off in Mukisa's head, and she reached up and held her eyes open with her hands, frantically pumping her legs to keep herself awake. She couldn't even tell which way was up now, and a panic began to build in her chest.

Suddenly a body eased its way into her path. Grimacing, she gave it a small nudge, and the body began to roll away from her, spinning to reveal a sallow face...

Mukisa's heart nearly stopped. It was Martin! But how could that be? His still body floated pathetically by, at a slow spin, his eyes closed. Mukisa's breath quickened. If he was still himself — if he hadn't transformed — then who was the specter?

She let out a soft moan and swam away from him, searching the vast emptiness before her for the others.

Her father was up ahead. She sped through the water to reach him, out of breath when she finally stopped by his side. He gripped her arm and held a finger up to his lips, eyes darting around. Mukisa listened carefully... a strained yell was coming from some direction, though she wasn't sure which.

She turned to see a small figure in the distance. It was Wyatt. They began to swim toward the boy, their ropes trailing out behind them from the change of direction.

They reached him just as John arrived from another direction. Wyatt prodded Mukisa on the shoulder and motioned frantically at a point to his right.

The four of them turned to watch a distant glowing object, too far to discern its shape, bobbing to and fro in the water like a fish. It slowly came closer and closer to them, and Mukisa's heart began crashing against her chest.

She instinctively reached out her left hand to take her father's, and felt something touch her right hand — it seemed that Wyatt had the same instincts. He gave her an apologetic look.

John, however, began swimming away. Mukisa scowled at him, and reached forward to grab him by the collar as he passed, halting his momentum. They exchanged looks, but Mukisa's was a little fiercer, and so, with a sulk, John fell into place beside them.

Wyatt was the first to actually move forward, toward the looming glow. The others followed behind slowly, preparing themselves for the worst. While it very well might not be the specter they were looking for, there was a very high probability that it was, and that put everyone on edge.

As the glow increased in size, Wyatt kept turning to make sure the others were behind him. Mukisa couldn't blame him; she was terrified too, and she was the one who had suggested coming down here in the first place. She absentmindedly touched the blade fitted neatly to her belt, finding the stony texture to be a comfort as they approached the beast. She could not wait to jab it into the specter's side, and get this nightmare over with... the sooner it was done, the sooner she could breathe, and really go looking for Cecilia and Paul. The others could swim to safety, and she hoped that they would immediately do so... but as for her, if she was down here already, she might as well be looking for her family.

Mukisa's eyelids were beginning to droop again, and that put her even more on edge. Worry began to creep into the corners of her mind that sleep would take them all before they even reached the beast, like it had clearly taken those who lay around them.

The glow started to reveal its form as they drew closer, and hopes and fears were simultaneously confirmed: it was definitely the specter. Mukisa's stomach turned violently when she saw what it was doing: its claws clamped onto a comatose victim, teeth sinking into the flesh, wings partially shielding the feeding frenzy from sight. Was this how it gained its strength, by feeding on its own kind?

Mukisa let out a cry, muffled by the water. It was not muffled enough, however, and the specter's head snapped up, its blood red eyes peering at the intruders shrewdly. It dropped the body, and eyed the four of them hungrily.

Mukisa's father shot her a look, as if to say, "Thanks a lot," and the four of them quickly backed away from the specter, huddling together in fear. Mukisa narrowed her eyes and motioned for them to spread out. Each of them pulled their weapons from their belts and began to circle around the beast.

Mukisa took a good look at the specter. It was huge compared to the specters they had seen in the sky; it actually looked about the size of a full grown man. Fangs protruded from its mouth, its thin lips rippling in a snarl around them, and its wings, massive and strong, flexed behind its shoulders, ready for action. Its skull bore chunks of long, wavy hair, which floated freely in the water; its face was gaunt and stern, with high cheekbones.

Mukisa's gaze moved on from its face, and she felt her heart sink into her stomach as she saw the jagged scar on its belly. She knew who the specter was. The bloodstained shirt must have long ago been discarded, but the wound still brought the memories flooding back. The specter locked eyes on her, those red eyes filled with a crazed recognition, and sneered.

The water around her suddenly felt heavier, less giving, as Mukisa took in the creature before her. His body was distorted, his face having become more like a beast's in the past five years, but it was definitely him. Mukisa was staring at the man she had pushed under the mud. She gripped her knife more tightly.

But it wasn't him anymore, was it? Yes, it was his body, and maybe it was even his mind buried in that head, just as depraved and vile as ever, but she wouldn't go so far as to call it Calam. However much of a beast he had been five years ago, it wasn't *him* anymore… it had now made its transformation complete. The old was gone, the new was here.

Its hungry gaze moved on to each of the others in turn, carefully sizing up its prey. Suddenly the specter let out a scream, and lunged toward Wyatt. The boy gasped, eyes wide, and brandished his spear, but it was clear that he wasn't even sure what to do with it. The specter reached him and easily dodged Wyatt's first jab, then rounded back and snatched the spear right from his hands.

Mukisa bolted forward, noting that John and Chancellor were doing the same, and hurriedly swam toward the specter, but none of them were quick enough. It reached forward, ensnaring Wyatt in its claws, and sunk its fangs into the boy's neck.

Mukisa screamed, and heard echoes from her companions around her. But her concern for Wyatt's wellbeing could come later — he had distracted the specter, albeit in the most morbid way possible, leaving its back turned to her. She reached the specter and grabbed at its wings, trying to steady herself as her knife shot forward, searching for skin. The specter arched its back to avoid the blade and swiveled around to give her a fiery glare; its wings flexed, and threw Mukisa backwards. She catapulted straight into John, knocking him back.

John's face was contorted with panic. "Wyatt!" he yelled, trying to push Mukisa away from him and swim to the boy.

The specter turned to greet Chancellor, clearly having lost interest in the cloud of blood forming around Wyatt's writhing body. Mukisa breathed a quick sigh of relief — he was moving, so he was still alive. She quickly turned her attention to her father, who was swinging his axe frantically at the beast. It was fast; it dove forward, dodging the blows as they came, and planted its hands firmly around the handle of the axe, inciting a tussle with Chancellor in an attempt to wrench it from his grasp.

Mukisa darted forward, again hoping to use the specter's preoccupation to her advantage. This time she tried to come from further below, slipping through the wings as they flexed upward, and she plunged her knife easily into the specter's lower back.

It shrieked, arching its spine, letting go of the axe and reaching around to grab Mukisa tightly by the neck in one fluid movement. The force from the specter's thrust sent Chancellor catapulting away through the water, still gripping the axe.

Mukisa felt the tendons in her neck struggling against the specter's grip. She quickly twisted the knife further into the specter's body, one last attempt before she felt her body being swung forward. The underwater world around her spun, and the specter's face came into view several inches from her own, grinning, mocking her with its memories. Gasping for air, she tried to pry its bony fingers from her throat. She could see dots in her line of vision, getting bigger and bigger, and her mind staggered back, five years rushing by until she could see him, see Calam; she was standing over his body, and his face kept flickering back and forth from specter blue to the color of humanity—

The specter let out a shrill scream, jolting Mukisa back to her place beneath the mud, and she watched with a mix of horror and fascination as its eyes began to shift, its irises crackling and transforming, chink by chink, from a blood red to an icy blue. The creature now looked exactly like an oversized version of the specters from the sky.

It looked up, toward the surface of the field. The look on its face was startling — it looked almost hopeful, and happy. It turned back to Mukisa and bared its fangs at her, moving in for the kill.

Suddenly, Mukisa felt her body lurching, being yanked backwards, and the specter shrieked as it struggled to maintain its grip around her neck, being pulled along with her. Mukisa saw the others in her peripheral vision, moving in the same direction, and was struck by understanding: the villagers were reeling them back in. She quickly lifted her arms and began striking at the specter's wrists, trying to break its hold on her throat, but the specter's grip was unrelenting. It clung to her, and she suddenly got the impression that the specter was no longer holding onto its prey — it was holding onto its transport. Its previous look of hope had transformed into a look of determination as they rushed toward the surface of the field.

"No!" she cried, but her strength was

failing her... she could do nothing as the two of them crashed through the wall of mud above them.

They burst out of the surface of the field, Mukisa still clawing at the hand around her throat. She watched helplessly as the specter's head crowned before her, its glow masked by the mud dripping from its body. But the wings gave it away — around them, the villagers holding the rope fell over themselves trying to gain distance from the beast.

Mukisa gasped for air as the specter relinquished its grip on her neck, turning its head upwards to the sky and letting out a piercing scream. She glanced at the horde of specters which had formed, circling overhead.

She was dimly aware of the people around her: her father had surfaced to her left, and John and Wyatt were to her right; John's arm was gripped tightly around Wyatt's torso, and Wyatt lay limp, his head lolled to one side. Beyond them, the entire village bordered the field, watching anxiously.

Mukisa returned her focus to the beast before her. It raised itself up, crouching over her shaking body, and reached back, roughly pulling the dagger from its back. It eyed the knife, glancing back and forth between it and Mukisa.

"Mukisa!" At the edge of the field, there was movement: her mother was running toward them. The specter quickly directed its attention toward her. For a split second Mukisa wondered if her mother would recognize the beast's face; but she seemed more concerned with Mukisa than with the specter. She couldn't recognize him if she wasn't expecting him.

Mukisa took advantage of her mother's distraction to swiftly kick out with both feet, one foot knocking the knife from its hands and the other planting itself firmly on the specter's chest. It toppled backwards, but the beast's wings balanced it out before it hit the mud.

Mukisa realized with horror that the specters in the sky were drawing nearer. They swooped down, and the beast let out a cry to greet them as they aimed for the field. Their responding cries wedged yet one more splinter of fear into her heart.

Sudden realization came to Mukisa: it wasn't towards her that they were diving. The specters circled around the beast, whose wounds were, thankfully, a detriment to its ability to fly.

She crept forward, one eye on the ring of specters, the other fixed determinedly on the half-sunken knife that lay next to them. She lunged for the knife, stirring the horde of specters up into the air briefly. But they stayed loyally by their new friend's side, assessing this new danger with beady little eyes.

Mukisa swung the knife, letting out a fierce cry as she did so, hoping to intimidate more than anything. She missed the specters, but her message was clear, and one of them lunged forward and flexed its wings, knocking her off kilter and sending her backward into the mud.

Momentarily stunned, she felt herself begin to sink. Looking up, she saw her mother hurry to her side, grabbing onto her to prevent her from being lost to the mud. She glanced back up at the ring of specters, swarming around this new beast like a gaggle of concerned mothers.

The beast struggled to its feet, letting out an eerie cry, and the horde of specters drew closer, murmuring to it. Mukisa watched as the beast let out one last ear-shattering cry, then grasped its comrades' bodies with its arms, being carried into the air as they began to lift up off of the field. The whole village watched as the horde soared into the sky, disappearing in the distance over the forest.

Mukisa stared at the sky, shaken. She had been worried that he would attack her family, her village… but his only concern was to join his new family. And the other specters were content to simply collect their new friend and leave it at that.

And just like that, Mukisa felt the whole of her body empty its reserve of adrenaline-fed strength. She slumped over, and her whole body began to shudder; she realized she was crying. She wasn't even sure what she was crying about… was it pain? Relief? Confusion? She realized she was saying something, and she immediately understood: she was saying the name of her sister, over and over, between sobs. She felt her mother pull her into her arms, cradling her, and buried her face into her shoulder.

There was another source of sobbing. It was John, huddled over Wyatt's body. The villagers around them got very quiet. They all realized one thing at the same time: Wyatt was not moving.

John was trying to resuscitate the boy, but to no avail. Wyatt lay still beneath him, lips parted, eyelids ringed with mud. John finally collapsed beside his body, his breathing shaky and uneven.

All was silent for a moment as the villagers stared at the volunteers, unsure of what to do. Then the earth began to shudder, and they helped each other arise from the mud and hurriedly made their way to the edge of the field.

The mud picked up its momentum and began to convulse, churning and bubbling; and then, the field collapsed back to its normal state, and all was still.

♦

Twelve rows of solemn figures stood amongst the mossy trees, robed in black, heads down. One by one each row filed to the front of the assembly, each mourner placing a wild rose on top of the casket.

The funeral was held in the forest between the Southern and Western Village, out of respect for the new friends that Wyatt had made. Marie stood in the fifth row, trying to monitor her breathing and grasping her rose tight in her hand. Her other hand was draped across Mukisa's shoulder, her own shoulder supporting the girl's head, as they listened to Chancellor Wallheart speak, his deep voice echoing through the forest.

"The events that have transpired over the last few weeks have been hard to take in," he began. "For those in the Southern Village, because you experienced them firsthand, and for those in the Western Village... you weren't able to experience the events, but you knew those who were affected even more than the ones who were there."

Chancellor eyed the crowd hesitantly for a moment, then cleared his throat. "It is a terrible thing that we have to do as a village, burying a loved one... And I know that my fellow Western Villagers have a very strong instinct to blame the Southern Village due to its history of unfortunate events. But let us remind ourselves that sometimes things happen beyond our control — beyond anyone's control.

"This is not a day of casting blame. This is a day of remembrance." Chancellor glanced over at Delilah Pine, the woman who had mothered Wyatt for the past ten years; she cried silently into a friend's shoulder. "Wyatt Pine was a perfect example of what an upright citizen should be: slow to anger, quick to love, and always trying to find a way that he could help. That's why he was a digger... he couldn't think of a better job than to pull people out of the mud, and give them a chance at life. Every person he met was an opportunity to spread warmth. And sometimes he couldn't understand why not everyone agreed with him on this... it frustrated him, and that was what defined Wyatt's bad days: the days that people fought with each other.

"So it didn't surprise me when he was the one who jumped at the opportunity to dig in the Southern Village. Not only could he be of help where help was greatly needed, but he could also meet new people, experience new things. And when he caught a glimpse of what was under the mud in this neighboring village, he knew he couldn't just sit back and watch the destruction unfold. He wanted to help, and help was what he did. He was the one who made the village aware of the danger beneath the field, and he was one of the first to volunteer when they decided to fight the beast. And he died..." He hesitated, turning his gaze downward as he spoke the words. "He died protecting his new friends, those who he had quickly come to love."

As Chancellor spoke, Marie stroked her daughter's hair, lost in thought. A lot of people did a lot of things for those they loved... she just wished that those circumstances wouldn't so often end in heartbreak. Chancellor had left behind a life in his old village to be with the one he loved, and it had left him with a confusing mess of death and accusation... it was no wonder he had fled. Mukisa had killed her grandfather in order to protect her mother, and she had spent years on the defense and full of self-doubt. And now Wyatt...

She had heard what the specter had been doing under the mud — feeding on the bodies of those unconscious. It had torn Wyatt apart down there, and now they were holding his funeral. Marie tried not to think about who else might have been torn to shreds under the field.

But that wasn't the only thing that was troubling her. It was Mukisa. She had been very quiet since her stint under the field, a kind of quiet that indicated she wasn't just mourning, but working something out. Marie worried that she would try something again; but Mukisa didn't seem restless. She just seemed unsure.

She had noticed her speaking in a hushed voice with Mama Nina a few times, and for that she was relieved... whatever she was troubled with, Mama Nina would take care of it far better than Marie could ever do. She just selfishly wished that it was her that Mukisa wanted to talk to.

She shook her head to clear her thoughts. She could worry about these things any other day; but today there were other things to attend to. As Chancellor said, this was a day of remembrance. Of mourning.

She noted that people were moving around her, and Mukisa squeezed her hand. "The ceremony's over," she whispered. Marie nodded.

The villages began to split to return to their homes. Uncertain gestures of kindness were exchanged; it was clear that both villages were warming up to the idea of reconciliation, but given the circumstances, it would take time. No one was quite ready to trust just yet.

"I'm glad that's over," Mukisa mumbled apologetically. "I never like funerals."

"No one ever does," a voice behind them said. They turned to see Mama Nina, her small smile trying to edge the sadness away from her eyes. "But it's the death part that I like the least," she continued, placing a hand on each of the women's shoulders. She studied their faces. "How are we feeling?"

Marie saw Chancellor approaching them from the front of the assembly, and struggled with the cold feeling that whisked through her body. She sighed, turning back to Mama. "Feeling like I need to go home and sleep," she stated simply.

"I think that's a good idea," Mama smiled. "But don't forget to say goodbye." She pushed them forward and disappeared into the crowd as Chancellor reached them.

"Marie," he said. "I just wanted you to know…"

"It's okay," she said. "What's done is done."

Chancellor blinked. "Well, actually… I

wanted to let you know that a handful of people are meeting tonight to discuss opening the pond up to the Southern Village, and installing a new set of pipes that would reach to your village square."

Mukisa's eyes lit up. It was the first time Marie had seen her look hopeful since Paul fell. "Really?!" she cried.

Chancellor held up a hand. "I'm not making any promises… but I did goad them into agreeing to it by saying Wyatt would've loved the idea."

Marie gave a small smile. It was exciting news, but she would show her excitement when she saw some follow-through. "Thank you, Sheriff."

Chancellor hesitated… he looked like he had one last thing to say. "I… I'm not going to return to your village to continue digging. I haven't given up on Cecilia being found, but I know your diggers are capable of handling things. And I feel that I may have been more trouble than I was help." Marie was not about to deny that, but kept her mouth shut. "But I would still like to be notified when she is found."

"Of course. I would not keep such knowledge from you."

"And one other thing…" Chancellor cleared his throat hesitantly, glancing at Mukisa. "I know that I did a pretty good job of quartering myself out of the family… but I'd still like to be able to spend some time with you. May I visit on occasion?"

Mukisa shrugged, suddenly shy. "Of course."

Chancellor nodded, his eyes smiling more than he allowed his lips to. He gave Marie one last glance — a glance that saw the mask go up, and showed understanding that distance was requested — and politely excused himself from their presence, allowing them to make their way back to the Southern Village.

"Mukisa," Marie said slowly as they began their walk, "I know these past few days have been overwhelming. If you ever need to talk, you realize I am here…"

Mukisa nodded slowly. "Okay, Mama."

"I know it's tough — both your sister and your husband are gone — but they will be found."

She gave her a thin smile. "Thanks, Mama."

"You've just been acting so quiet…"

Mukisa rolled her eyes. "I *know*, Mama. It's been a rough week."

"I just..." Marie cleared her throat, giving a weak smile. "I don't want you to end up like me. You've got plenty of life ahead of you, and I don't want you to waste it staring out at that field, like I stared over my shoulder."

Mukisa stopped short, glaring at her. But her anger wasn't quite what Marie expected. "Why do you act as if your life is over, Mama? You always say, 'You won't end up like me, your life isn't ruined' — give it a rest! You are above the mud, Mama! You have been rescued from a fate that many weren't able to—" She hesitated, looking at the ground. "You're already better off than some."

Marie stared at her, startled. "I — I'm sorry. I didn't mean to—"

"What a surprise," Mukisa bristled. "You're taking the blame again." She sighed. "Mama... You told me that who I want to be says something about who I am." She stared into Marie's eyes. "And I aim to take that to heart. Maybe if you listened to yourself once in a while, you wouldn't feel so guilt-ridden all the time. But I guess you can spout off any old heartfelt piece of advice and still not learn from it yourself. Now, if you want to just pretend that everything that went wrong in your life is all your fault, then go damn right ahead. But I'll have nothing to do with it."

Mukisa stormed off, leaving Marie to stare after her, wondering where in the world that had all come from.

◆

A few days later, the ban on the field was lifted. The diggers went back to work hesitantly at first, but they had seen very little of the specters in the days following the accident, as they now called it, and the field seemed to be much more docile than normal... there were no issues pulling newcomers up. It seemed that everything had gone back to normal.

That is, except for Mukisa. She mustered up her strength and assigned herself the task of rebuilding what seemed like her entire life. Hunting was her constant, the one thing that she knew would not change. But to her, everything else had transformed right before her eyes. She now saw through the perspective of the field. Mama Nina had passed the burden of secrets down to her, and it was a heavy burden... not unbearable, but heavy.

But the burden did not change the way of life for the rest of the village. The day-to-day jobs were still the same: the diggers still needed to pull up newcomers, and room had to be made in the village for growth. While the rest of the village wondered what day would be best to harvest the crops, Mukisa sat thinking about how long it would take for her sister and husband to be affected by the field.

Her solace was in the fact that the field was still peaceful. Martin had had *years* more time under the mud than her family members... and his eyes had just turned red. There was hope, she thought.

But it was still hard to keep away from the field at night, to leave the fate of her family in the hands of the diggers. To remember that it was not up to her.

The villagers were very supportive; more

and more of them began to initiate conversation with the young woman, at first to express their condolences, and then to comment on the weather; and as time went by, Mukisa found that she had finally begun to feel more at ease in her own home.

Chancellor visited about once a month. He kept his visits short and to the point, catching up with his daughter during strolls in the shallow parts of the forest, and briefly saying hello to Marie as she patrolled the field. Marie was always grateful that he said hello, and equally grateful that he didn't dwell. Chancellor also tried to bring news from the other villages when he could, knowing that the Southern Village didn't get much in the way of town gossip.

About two months after Wyatt's death, the Western Village opened up their lake to the Southern Village to share. Plans for a pipe system that would reach the Southern Village were being devised. It was agreed that Wyatt would have been glad of this truce that had been made between the two villages.

One morning, several months after the accident, one of the diggers reached into the mud and uncovered Paul, quickly pulling him to safety. But it wasn't just Paul… his fingers were tightly grasped around a small wrist, and reinforcements were called over to uncover a second body — a little girl, with dark skin and tight curls.

A runner was immediately sent with

instructions to find the families and give the good news.

Marie was sitting in the Guest House on the edge of her bed, waiting patiently for the children to wake up. Looking to her left, she saw a little blonde head of hair smiling at her, with twinkling eyes and a giggle. It was one of the newcomers who had been unearthed just yesterday.

Marie stood up and crossed the room, kneeling at the little girl's bedside. "Have you decided on a name?"

"Shirley, I think."

"Shirley is a beautiful name." Marie smiled at her. "You're a happy little girl, aren't you?"

Shirley laughed. "Why wouldn't I be?"

"No nightmares, then?"

Shirley gave her a confused look, and Marie bit her lip thoughtfully. She glanced out the window and saw a young man bolting toward the door of the Guest House, a grin plastered across his face. She stood up, her heart suddenly clamoring, and smiled down at the little girl. "Welcome to the Southern Village, Shirley."

Acknowledgements

I know it's cheesy, but it must be said: stories can't just be told by one person. I've learned this in my filmmaking jaunts, as countless people put their hands on an idea that may have sprouted from my brain but grew due to the love and passion of those around me.

And the same goes for novel writing... it seems bizarre that this could be true for a piece of writing with a single author, but without the people around me to bounce ideas off of and tweak details, *The Fields* would've been dead in the water.

And so I must give a special thank you to my family, who endured the countless texts and phone calls about character arcs and structure mishaps through the long process of this novel, especially towards the end (I'm talking especially about you, Mom and Becky! Love, love). You know more than anyone how annoyingly obsessive I can be once I get going, and yet you put up with me, and I cannot appreciate that enough.

Thank you to the people in my writing group way back when for putting up with an evolving story idea — especially Cassidy Atkins and Janet Somes, who stuck with the story meeting after meeting. I owe a lot to Paul Barker and Hal Cramer, who each sat with me on separate occasions and picked my brain about different plot ideas and world-building details as I wrestled with the story. Thanks to Delaney, Steve McHale, Ashley Mahdavi, Cliff Ash, Pat McBride, and Brandon Rexrode in getting excited about my story and sharing their notes with me.

And a very special thank you to Mr. Whinnem (I will never get used to calling him anything else!), who taught me a love of story in high school and is always a reminder of what I can accomplish with a little passion. If it hadn't been for Writer's Forum, and the encouragement you gave, I probably never would have started writing this book... it took me long enough, but I finally got there, and I have you to thank for it.

About The Author

Sammi Leigh Melville lives in Harrisburg, PA with her cat, Loren. She has written and directed several short films through her production company, Screaming Pictures, and is the program director for Vidjam, a non-profit organization which works to encourage and foster filmmaking in the Central PA area. You may see her on the weekends at the Harrisburg Improv Theater, performing long-form improv with one of her troops. Sammi has a strange sense of humor, a fervent love for both people and nature, and an awkward tendency to get real deep when no one is expecting it.